"I don't want you to regret last night."

Matt knew it wasn't as simple as that. People would talk. All the more reason to get rid of the story as soon as possible.

She sighed and her shoulders dropped in defeat. "I know that, but it doesn't matter. We can't let this happen again. There are too many prying eyes. It could destroy us both."

Matt knew she was right. He just wished he wasn't so disappointed by the truth. If he could have anything right now, it was her. "I won't let that happen."

"See? Power. You can control this. I can't."

He brushed her cheek with the back of his hand. He knew he shouldn't touch her, but the way she subtly pressed against his hand sent the blood coursing through his body. "If you understood how badly I want you right now, you would know that the power is all yours."

* * *

Tempted by Scandal is the first book of the Dynasties: Secrets of the A-List quartet.

Dear Reader,

Thanks for picking up *Tempted by Scandal*! It's the first book in the new Dynasties: Secrets of the A-List series. The books to follow are *Taken by Storm* by Cat Schield, *Seduced by Second Chances* by Reese Ryan and *Redeemed by Passion* by Joss Wood. The four of us will transport you to a sexy and exciting world of money and power set against the beautiful backdrop of Seattle and the Pacific Northwest.

My story revolves around Matt and Nadia, who are boss and assistant. Matt is the affable golden boy who's rarely denied anything he wants until Nadia comes along. Nadia is incredibly fierce and determined, having lived her whole life judged for her beauty rather than her brains. When a tabloid scandal hits, Nadia has every reason to run away from Matt as fast as she can, but her heart won't let her.

Cat, Reese, Joss and I got to work very closely on this series, trading notes and exchanging ideas to connect our four stories. Also in the mix was Harlequin Desire senior editor Stacy Boyd, who helped us pull everything together. Working with the Harlequin editorial team and my fellow Desire authors is one of the best parts of writing for Harlequin. I feel so lucky every chance I have to do it.

I hope you enjoy the start of Dynasties: Secrets of the A-List! Drop me a line anytime at karen@karenbooth.net. I love hearing from readers!

Karen

KAREN BOOTH

TEMPTED BY SCANDAL

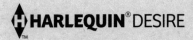

Special thanks and acknowledgment are given to Karen Booth for her contribution to the Dynasties: Secrets of the A-List miniseries.

ISBN-13: 978-1-335-60364-7

Tempted by Scandal

Copyright © 2019 by Harlequin Books S.A.

This edition published by arrangement with Harlequin Books S.A.

For questions and comments about the quality of this book, please contact us at CustomerService@Harlequin.com.

Printed in U.S.A.

Karen Booth is a Midwestern girl transplanted to the South, raised on '80s music and repeated readings of *Forever...* by Judy Blume. When she takes a break from the art of romance, she's listening to music with her nearly grown kids or sweet-talking her husband into making her a cocktail. Learn more about Karen at karenbooth.net.

Books by Karen Booth

Harlequin Desire

The Best Man's Baby
The Ten-Day Baby Takeover
Snowed in with a Billionaire

The Eden Empire

A Christmas Temptation
A Cinderella Seduction

Dynasties: Secrets of the A-List

Tempted by Scandal

Visit her Author Profile page at Harlequin.com, or karenbooth.net, for more titles.

You can find Karen Booth on Facebook, along with other Harlequin Desire authors, at Facebook.com/harlequindesireauthors!

For Cat Schield, Reese Ryan and Joss Wood,
my incredible Desire sisters.

* * *

Don't miss a single book in the
Dynasties: Secrets of the A-List quartet!

Tempted by Scandal by Karen Booth
Taken by Storm by Cat Schield
Seduced by Second Chances by Reese Ryan
Redeemed by Passion by Joss Wood

One

Nadia Gonzalez didn't believe in regrets. She simply did her damnedest to never make a mistake. Being careful but determined always paid off—that approach got her into the college she wanted to attend and a scholarship for the tuition she couldn't afford. When she was younger, her resoluteness had helped her win several beauty pageants—not her proudest achievements but ones that had meant a great deal to her mother. More recently, her perseverance had helped her land her job as executive admin for Matt Richmond, one of the wealthiest and most powerful men in the world. That was the real feather in her cap and she wasn't about to do anything to put that at risk.

But there was a very good chance that Nadia had

gown she'd donned for the hospital fund-raiser. Leaving that early had been Matt's suggestion and Nadia agreed. He was an incredibly powerful man and men like him drew attention. Neither of them could afford the optics of a boss-assistant tryst, but especially not Matt. There were too many people eager to tear him down. That's what happens when you have success mere mortals can't begin to comprehend.

"Great," Nadia said. "I'm heading in to meet with him right now." The thought of seeing Matt was making the thighs-on-fire situation that much more intense. "Be sure to take good care of my car. It's my baby."

"Of course, Ms. Gonzalez." The valet hopped into her month-old silver Audi, a bonus from Matt for a job well done on the still-secret Sasha project, a joint partnership between Matt and Liam Christopher, his best friend from college. Nadia had worked hard for that car. She'd earned it.

But thinking about crossing the line with Matt while watching her prized car disappear into a parking garage made her question her priorities. Yes, she'd wanted Matt for a long time and they'd shared an unbelievable night of passion. But so what? Was she really willing to throw away her career and quite possibly the most primo admin job in the US? No. Was she willing to discount the years she'd scraped by so she could make a better life for herself and her family? Absolutely not. A guy like Matt was not the settling-down type. There would be no happy ending with him. Which meant that her first priority when speaking to him today would be to make sure he understood that last night was a one-time thing. They would both be better off if they forgot about it and returned to their strictly professional dynamic, even though that was going to break her heart.

Nadia made her way up the flagstone promenade to the massive double doors of the main lodge. Two doormen in smart black jackets opened them in unison, and she swept into the grand but warm lobby. Every detail was perfect—mahogany wood moldings, high ceilings and elegant chandeliers. She'd spent a lot of time in surroundings like this since she'd started working with Matt, far removed from her modest upbringing in Chino, California, outside Los Angeles. It felt good to be in this world. She liked being able to help pay her younger sister's college tuition, and chip away at her mother's medical bills so her parents could sleep easier at night. All the more reason to hold on to her job tightly and put Matt back in a box with a note saying, "He's your boss. Don't be stupid."

Nadia arrived at the front desk and gave her name. As the clerk checked the computer, Nadia's phone beeped with a text from Matt.

Come up when you arrive. 310. Meeting with Teresa St. Claire at 2:00.

"Yes," the clerk said. "Ms. Gonzalez, we have you in room three-twelve. Right next to Mr. Richmond."

Nadia smiled and swallowed hard, swiping the keycard from the gleaming wood counter. Nothing like staying next door to the man you can't resist. "Fantastic."

"Elevators are at the far side of the lobby. I'll have a bellhop bring up your bag."

"Thank you." Nadia hustled over and jabbed the button then typed out a quick response to Matt on her phone. On my way.

Good. A single word was his only response, a stark reminder that he was an impossibly busy man who always put business first.

The trip up three floors was just long enough to sort out what she had to say to Matt. Today would mark the end of their personal involvement. They had to put a stop to it before it went too far.

At the very end of the long hall, she passed by her door and knocked on his, staring down at her feet, choking back the anticipation of seeing him again. She would not falter. She would be the picture of capable and confident, even when she was feeling nothing more than weak. She would shrug off their tryst, let Matt off the hook and move on. She was too smart and had worked too hard to give herself anything less.

Matt Richmond looked out the windows of his hotel suite, allowing himself to be momentarily entranced by the sight of Centennial Falls. This was one of the calling cards of The Opulence—the main building was precariously perched at the edge of the stories-high drop. He watched as ice-cold water rushed, churned and poured over the rocky ledge, leaving behind only mist and spray. Mother Nature was one of the only things that amazed him anymore. Everything man-made could be explained. He liked the mystery. He liked that he couldn't control it.

Honestly, that was part of the appeal of Nadia. On the outside, she was unflappable. A beautiful closed book. But he'd sensed that on the inside was a woman untamed. That inkling had made him play with fire. The thought of having her in his bed sent a ripple of heat right through him. It was as if the fire was still here.

He jumped when the knock came at the door. *Nadia.* He'd spent hours trying to decide how to handle their working relationship now. He'd determined his only course was to let her lead the way. He bounded across the room and opened the door. She regularly knocked the breath out of him, but today her effect on him was even stronger.

"Mr. Richmond." Without making eye contact, Nadia swept into the room and set her purse and laptop bag down on the coffee table, then strode over to the desk. She immediately began straightening the papers he'd left strewn about. "You've been busy."

He followed her, walking through the heavenly wake of her perfume. Her wavy blond hair was up in a twist and he caught himself wanting to pull it out.

Instead he stuffed his hands into his pockets. "You don't have to do that."

"You have a very busy day and you work better when you're organized."

He couldn't help but smile. "You know me better than I know myself."

"It's my job to know you." She turned and finally looked at him, but her eyes weren't warm and inviting like they'd been last night. Now they were full of worry. "Which makes me wonder what you were thinking when you had the hotel put me in the room next to yours. That doesn't seem like a good idea."

"What? I had no idea. You made the reservation."

"And the Richmond Hotel Group manages the hotel." She took in a deep breath. "Look, Mr. Richmond…"

He reached out and placed his hand on her arm. The connection to her was immediate. He craved her the way he needed to breathe. "You're going to call me Mr. Richmond now? After the things we did together? We're alone, Nadia. Please, call me Matt."

"Fine. Matt. Last night was a mistake."

That word sliced through him. The only mistakes he ever made were in trusting the wrong people. Had he slipped up by trusting her?

"We both need to forget it ever happened," she continued.

That didn't sit well with him, either. "That's going to be a difficult task when I go home tomorrow and climb into bed and realize my sheets smell like you."

"So have one of your ten housekeepers change them."

Matt didn't enjoy having his success thrown in his face. It wasn't his fault he was successful or rich. From the desk, his phone rang. Nadia turned and picked it up, glancing at the screen.

"It's Shayla." Shayla Jerome was Richmond Industries' head of Public Relations.

"Is this important?" Matt answered. "I'm in the middle of something."

"Yes, it's important. We have a situation on our hands."

Matt hated the way Shayla couched every bit of news she had to deliver. "Please spit it out. I don't have time for this. If there's a fire, get out the extinguishers."

She cleared her throat. "Fine. *TBG* just posted pictures of your beauty-queen admin leaving your house in the middle of the night wearing the gown she'd been photographed wearing hours earlier at the hospital benefit."

Matt's stomach sank. *The Big Gossip*, or *TBG*, was a tabloid website with an unsavory reputation and a massive following. He ran his hands through his hair. Nadia glanced over at him and her eyes narrowed. Nadia had an uncanny ability to read him and he wasn't ready to share this bit of news with her. He turned and walked away. "How did this happen?"

"That's not really a question for me now, is it?

I'm guessing that somebody on your security detail fell down on the job. Or more likely, fell asleep."

A low rumble escaped Matt's throat. "Fine. I'll talk to Phil."

"That only helps with preventing this from happening again. For now we have a story trending about you sleeping with an employee. It does not look good."

"So kill it."

"*TBG* has new ownership and a whole new editorial team. They're not about to bend to the whim of a publicist."

"Then offer them something better."

That was enough to get Nadia to walk over to where he was standing by the windows, her flawless face full of worry. He did enjoy the way her full lips went slack. "What's going on?" she whispered.

Matt merely shook his head.

"Access to the Saturday night gala during the retreat?" Shayla asked.

Matt had refused *TBG*'s request for access. That retreat was meant to be an exclusive weekend-long getaway for the business elite and Matt's closest celebrity friends. People came to a party like that to have fun outside the public eye. "Is there another way?"

"I can deny the story and make something up. Say there was a work emergency and you had to go straight to your house from the fund-raiser. You needed Nadia's help and it was closer than the office."

Matt thought it through for a second. "That could work."

"Oh, my God," Nadia said, looking at her phone. She showed him the screen. There was the story. And that horrible headline, plain as day: "Beauty and the Boss?" Whoever had taken the picture of her tiptoeing her way out of his house had used a camera with night-vision technology.

"I need Nadia to sign a nondisclosure agreement before I do this, though," Shayla said. "Richmond Industries can't afford to have her turn around and decide to sell her story to the highest bidder."

Matt's stomach was done dropping and was now angrily churning. "I don't think that's necessary."

"Do you trust her implicitly? Because I don't."

"You don't trust anyone."

"A man in your position shouldn't, either. For all we know, Nadia tipped off that photographer."

Matt refused to believe Nadia was capable of that. "Just take care of it. Please." With that, Matt ended the call.

Nadia's wide eyes were pleading. "Is this why Shayla called?" She glanced down at her phone in disgust and handed it to him. "We have to do something. I don't want my coworkers knowing that I slept with you."

Matt hated that the memory of his amazing night with Nadia had now been eclipsed by a pulpy story, but at least he knew that Nadia had not played a role in the photographer's presence. If she had, she wouldn't be so upset right now. "I told Shayla to kill it. Don't worry about it. It will go away."

"It's so easy for you to say that. You have all the power here. I'm nobody." Nadia wrapped her arms around her waist and turned to the window overlooking the falls.

He hated hearing her refer to herself that way. She wasn't nobody to him. And looking at her right now, all he could think about was how badly he wanted her. It made it nearly impossible to think straight. "Nadia." He put his hand on her shoulder and watched as she turned and looked back at him, her warm brown eyes inviting him in. "I don't want you to regret the things we did together. We're two consenting adults." Matt knew it wasn't as simple as that. People would talk. All the more reason for Shayla to get rid of the story as soon as possible.

She sighed and her shoulders dropped in defeat. "I know that, but it doesn't matter. We can't let this happen again. There are too many prying eyes. It could destroy us both."

Nadia was right. Matt only wished he wasn't so disappointed by the truth. If he could have anything he wanted right now, it would be her. "I won't let that happen."

"See? Power. You can control this. I can't."

He brushed her cheek with the back of his hand. He knew he shouldn't, but the way she subtly pressed against his touch sent the blood coursing through his body. "If you understood how badly I want you right now, you would know that the power is all yours."

Two

Teresa St. Claire's heart hammered at the thought of what was only ten or fifteen minutes away, but she took several deep breaths and reminded herself that this was exactly what she'd worked so hard for. Meeting with billionaire businessman Matt Richmond would be intimidating for anyone—few people in the world had as much money and influence as he did—but he was also her client. *Her client*. Her dreams were coming true. She was here to plan Richmond Industries' fifth-anniversary extravaganza. She was here to make Matt Richmond happy, and she would rock it so hard he'd never hire another event planner in his entire life.

The young man running the valet stand rushed

to Teresa's door and opened it. He flashed a warm smile, and her nerves settled. "Checking in, miss?" he asked.

She left the keys in the ignition and eased out of the car. "I am. Just for the night right now, but you'll see a lot of me over the next five weeks." She held out her hand. "Teresa St. Claire. Limitless Events. I'm planning the Richmond retreat."

"I'm Michael." He cocked his head to the side, face full of surprise. Perhaps he wasn't accustomed to guests introducing themselves, but Teresa made a habit of knowing everyone by name. That's how you got things done. Plus, he reminded Teresa of her younger brother, Joshua, whom she missed terribly and hadn't seen in months. "I'll have the bellman take your suitcase up to your room. Let me know if you need anything at all, Ms. St. Claire."

"Nice to meet you, Michael. I'm sure I'll see you around." Teresa hooked her navy leather Fendi bag on her arm, straightened her black peplum jacket and marched into The Opulence. The lobby was stunning, but Teresa was already brainstorming ideas to make it better for the retreat. It was an automatic shift in thinking. Her training with Mariella Santiago-Marshall at MSM Event Planning in Santa Barbara had served her well. Mr. Richmond and his guests would be taking over the entire resort and Teresa wanted them to step into an event they would talk about for years. That was how she'd cement Limitless Events' spot on the map. Billionaires, business moguls and celebrities from all over the world would know her name.

Teresa stopped at the front desk, and the clerk led her through the lobby, past the bar and down a hall to a meeting room. The space was modest but stately, with a gleaming wood conference table for six and a seating area with beautifully upholstered chairs poised in front of a wide picture window. She wandered over to admire the view of Centennial Falls. Sitting in a front-row seat was the ideal place to meet with Mr. Richmond so she could paint the picture of his perfect event. Mariella Santiago-Marshall had taught her that—tell the client a story, let them imagine their guests stepping into a world unlike anything they've ever experienced. That's how you made memories, and memories were how you made lifelong clients.

She was about to sit in one of the chairs when her cellphone rang with a call from her assistant, Corinne Donovan. "Hey," Teresa answered. "I only have a minute. Matt Richmond should be here soon."

"Did you not get my messages?"

"No. What messages?"

"I left you three voice mails."

"There's a dead zone between Seattle and The Opulence. I'm sure I lost cell service. What's wrong? You sound frazzled."

"A man has been calling the office for you. He won't tell me his name. He kept asking for your cell number and I didn't want to give it to him, but then he said it was urgent so I finally just did. He said it's life or death."

Goose bumps raced over Teresa's skin. "Is he going to call me?" Before Corinne could answer, Teresa heard the beep telling her that she had a call on the other line. "This must be him. I'd better take this."

"Call me when you get a chance. I'm worried."

So am I. "I'll fill you in when I can." Teresa ended the call and answered again. "Hello?"

"Ms. St. Claire." Despite Corinne's report of this being a life-or-death situation, the man's voice was careful and measured, as if he had all the time in the world.

"This is Teresa. Who's calling?"

"I'm a messenger. I'm calling about Joshua."

Teresa's blood ran cold. By design, very few people knew about her younger brother. "What about him?" She hated that defensive tone in her voice, but it came out by pure instinct. She would do anything to protect Joshua.

"Your brother has a habit of getting into trouble, doesn't he?"

Teresa wasn't going to answer that question. Yes, Joshua had gotten himself into quite a mess a few years ago in Las Vegas, but she'd gotten all of that cleared up via The Fixer, a longtime associate of Mariella Santiago-Marshall's husband, Harrison. The Fixer did exactly what his moniker suggested—he made problems go away. "What do you want?"

"Joshua owes some very important people and he's not going to be able to weasel his way out of it."

"Owes what?"

"With interest, seven million dollars. Payable now."

Teresa's heart nearly stopped. What could Joshua have done that would get him into that deep a hole? "Joshua doesn't have that kind of money."

"Which is why I went to the person who cares most about keeping him alive."

Teresa's stomach lurched. "That's preposterous. I don't have that kind of money, either."

"Hunter Price invested in your company. He's a wealthy man. Surely he gave you something to put away."

It truly terrified her that this man knew these details of her life. Her agreement with Hunter had been nothing but discreet. Yes, he had invested in Limitless, but those funds had gone right into the business, for office space, staffing and outfitting the entire operation. "I don't have seven million dollars."

"Then come up with it."

"How, exactly?"

"Not my problem. Just keep in mind that Joshua is running out of time."

"Don't you dare hurt him."

The man laughed, a sickening sound that told her he was no stranger to harming people. Teresa couldn't believe this nightmare was happening again. A cocktail of anger and guilt mixed inside her. She'd always been Joshua's protector. She'd practically been his mother. Their own mother, Talisa, was scattered and overwhelmed by the world, although it was hard even now to blame her. She'd done her best as a single mom. Nothing had been right after Teresa and Joshua's father, Nigel, died.

"I'm a reasonable man. I won't hurt him right away," the man continued. "First, I air Joshua's dirty laundry. See how badly that hurts your business. You work with some very wealthy, important people. I'm sure they'd love to learn what your little brother did in Vegas. Your brother that you practically raised. The brother you're supposed to be guiding through life."

Teresa swallowed hard. Her eyes darted to the window, but the sight of the millions of gallons of water rushing over the rocky drop of Centennial Falls was no longer beautiful. It made her even queasier. None of this was fair. She'd worked hard to help Joshua on track. She'd only needed to see him in jail once before she'd become fully committed to keeping him out.

But the truth was that since she'd started Limitless and moved back to Seattle, she'd been laser-focused on her career. She hadn't been keeping close tabs on Joshua. Every time they'd spoken, Joshua assured her he was doing fine. Now she knew he wasn't exactly keeping his nose clean. She should've been paying closer attention.

"I'm sure your clients will be especially surprised to find out what his big sister did to make it go away."

Teresa's pulse pounded. She quickly glanced at the meeting-room door. No sign of Matt Richmond and that was a good thing. Still, she did not want to risk him walking in while she was having this conversation. Her nerves were too frayed. "Look. I'm going to need time to figure this out. I don't have that kind of cash available." If nothing else, she needed to verify that this was actually true. A big part of her wanted to give Joshua the benefit of the doubt. "I need your number so I can get back to you. The call came through as 'unknown.'"

"That's not how this works. You should know that by now. I'll be in touch." The line went dead.

A tall, broad figure stepped into her peripheral vision. *Oh, God. Matt Richmond.* She took a deep breath, smiled and rose from her seat, only to be confronted by an image plucked from her past, a man she'd only dreamed of running into. Liam Christopher.

For a moment, she and Liam stared at each other. He was even easier on the eyes now than the last time she'd seen him. Six years ago? Seven? His square jaw and the dark scruff along it suited him so well. His green eyes were as piercing as ever. Right now, they were almost too intense.

"What are you doing here?" His voice boomed in the small space.

He must not recognize her. That was the only

reason his voice would be dripping with contempt. She stepped closer and offered her hand. "Liam. Hi. Teresa St. Claire. We've met a few times. Your father was my mentor when I was in business school."

He looked at her hand as if he couldn't be any more repulsed by the idea of touching her. "You think I don't know who you are? As if I could forget. Tell me what you're doing here."

She didn't understand the anger in his voice, but her first instinct was to tell him everything he wanted to know. Perhaps that would calm him down so she could figure out why he was so agitated. "I'm waiting for Matt Richmond. He and I have a meeting scheduled to take place in this room. I'm surprised to see you, but you two are close friends, aren't you?"

"What do you want with Matt?"

Now her patience was wearing thin. There were too many unpleasant things coming out of Liam's stunning mouth. "I'm sorry, but did I miss something? I haven't seen you in six years? Seven? And you march into my meeting all angry?"

"*Your* meeting? I have a meeting with Matt. And I can guarantee you that whatever it is that you think you're going to be talking to him about, I'll be putting a quick end to it."

Nobody messed with her and her business. She was not going to lose this event, especially not when she might have to come up with an exorbitant sum of money to save her brother again. "I don't know why Mr. Richmond double-booked himself, but he's not here, so we're both going to have to wait. Perhaps you can take this time to tell me why you're so upset with me." She pulled back a chair from the conference table and offered it. "Here. Have a seat. Let's talk."

Liam shook his head, his jaw visibly tighter. "Stop playing games."

Teresa felt her own anger about to eclipse Liam's. "Games? I'm playing games? How about you tell me why you're so mad at me."

Liam shook his head again, this time slowly and steadily. It felt as if his eyes might bore a hole right through her. "You know what you did. You ruined my father's life."

Liam Christopher had imagined many times what he might say to Teresa St. Claire if he ever ran into her, but he'd failed to take into account just how badly his temper would flare. He normally played things exceptionally close to the vest, but evidently all bets were off with Teresa.

"Ruined his life? Your father was my mentor." Her pleading tone only made her that much more unlikable. "I've always cared deeply about him. He helped me get my start in business. I have no idea what you're talking about."

"Don't play coy with me. It's insulting." Tension spread across his shoulders and back like a sickness. Although it had been seven years since he last saw Teresa, he would never forget her. Not because she was beautiful, although she was regrettably gorgeous—

tall and willowy with long blond hair and striking blue eyes. She was apparently the sort of woman his father had a weakness for. Teresa St. Claire had convinced his father to stray outside his marriage. She was the reason his parents split. She was the reason his mother's heart had been irrevocably shattered.

"I honestly have no idea what you're talking about."

Teresa was either in denial or the type of person who would willingly lie to make herself look good. He had no patience for either. He cleared his throat and stuffed his hands into his pockets. Where was Matt? Liam wanted nothing more than to let his best friend know whom he was about to meet with so he could have Teresa escorted from the building and, hopefully, his life.

"What are you and Mr. Richmond meeting about today?" she asked.

"Not that I owe you an explanation, but we're announcing a partnership during his retreat."

"Maybe that's why Matt double-booked his time. I'm organizing the entire event. Perhaps he wanted us to discuss the details."

This was *not* happening. "You can wager as many guesses as you want, but it's not going to matter. Matt and I have been best friends since college. We are each other's closest confidants. You won't be organizing anything I'm involved with. And I also won't let you take advantage of my best friend."

Teresa visibly winced. A part of him was glad he

could get to her like this, but he took no real pleasure in making threats. He only knew that he could not work with Teresa. His partnership with Matt's company on the Sasha artificial-intelligence project had been years and millions of dollars in the making. Plus, he had to let Matt know whom he was dealing with.

"Is there some sort of jealousy here? Are you upset that your father helped me all those years ago? I realize he went above and beyond what most mentors might do, but we were very close. He believed in me."

Jealousy? Teresa had a real talent for twisting things back on other people. "Jealous is the last thing I am. More like disgusted." Liam turned his back to Teresa and spotted Matt making his way down the hall. Liam met him at the doorway. "We have to talk about her."

"Mr. Richmond, whatever he's about to say, I can explain." Teresa was right behind Liam, craning her neck over his shoulder to get a glimpse of Matt. The desperation in her voice reeked of false drama. There was no explaining away what she'd done, and she knew it.

"Matt, you trust me, right?" Liam asked.

"Of course." Matt looked beyond bewildered, which wasn't an expression Liam had seen many times on his friend's face. Matt was the calm and collected guy with his finger on the pulse of everything. It was impossible to catch him by surprise, which was part of the reason Matt and Liam had hit it off the very first day they met. They both prided themselves on being unflappable. They simply pulled it off in very different ways.

Liam glanced over at Teresa. Her vivid blue eyes were wide, darting back and forth between Matt and him. It would have been so easy to cut her off at the knees, but Liam wasn't going to let her off the hook so easy. She could try to explain herself to Matt. "Whatever you've hired her to do, whatever business arrangement you two have, you'll do yourself a favor if you end it right here. She can't be trusted."

"Mr. Richmond, I have no earthly idea what Liam is talking about. And whatever he may think of me, I assure you that has no bearing on my abilities as an event planner."

Matt shook his head, still seeming confused. He turned to Liam. "Do you want to tell me what's going on?"

"She and I have a history. Or more specifically, she and my father. But I think you should have her explain it." *Every dirty detail.*

Matt sighed and pulled Liam aside. "Look, she and I are weeks into planning the retreat. I'd rather not throw all of that work away. This event is already taking on a life of its own. Give me a chance to meet with her and I'll catch up with you later, okay?"

Liam knew Matt had a point. Letting business and personal matters intermingle was never a good idea. Matt was a stickler for keeping the two things separate. Liam was as well, but he was apparently having a weak moment. Maybe he simply needed to go outside and clear his head. "Yeah. Of course." Liam turned to look at Teresa one more time. He expected to see her gloating, but she looked worried. Good. Let her suffer at least a few repercussions. With nothing left to say, he stalked out into the hall.

He headed for the bar just beyond the lobby. It had a large balcony overlooking the falls. He looked forward to a shot of autumn air to clear his head, but every step away from his altercation with Teresa left him feeling more foolish, and that in turn only made him more angry. He knew he shouldn't let his emotions get to him, but the matter of Teresa was a complicated one.

The night Liam had first met Teresa, he couldn't have been any more entranced and enchanted. His father had asked him to dinner at the house, the Christopher family estate on the west side of Mercer Island. His father hadn't made note of the occasion, only saying that he had a promising student in the class he was teaching at the University of Washington, his alma mater. Liam hadn't wanted to attend the dinner. He was twenty-five by then, fully independent and making a name for himself within the family company. Plus, he knew exactly what was going to happen at dinner that night. His father would start to drink too much and would begin regaling their esteemed guest with tales of business conquests and billions made. Liam and his mother, Catherine, would exchange pained smiles and endure it. Liam didn't begrudge his father his success. He only disliked his obsession with it. Nothing was ever enough.

Much to Liam's surprise, that night's dinner guest was a breath of fresh air. Yes, his father was being a bit of a boastful blowhard during the meal. But Teresa St. Claire was as charming and beautiful a woman as Liam had ever seen. She was smart as a whip, with a wit that made him laugh more than once. She had a broad range of interests, was keenly focused on business and was nothing but eager to take on the world. No wonder his father was so enamored of her. Liam was as well. In fact, he'd never encountered a woman quite like her—an unparalleled beauty, sexy and enticing, but wholly enthralled with the business world. By the time dessert was served, Liam was convinced that meeting Teresa was fate. She was his perfect woman. At the end of the night, he walked her out to her car and made his move.

"It was so nice to meet you," she'd said, offering her hand.

Liam could hardly think straight when her skin touched his—there was an unmistakable zap of electricity between them. He'd gazed down into her deep blue eyes, made even more complex and intriguing in the soft evening light. "I really enjoyed meeting you. I'd love to see you again. Would you like to have dinner next week? Just the two of us?

There's an amazing new seafood place downtown. The St. James?"

Surprise crossed Teresa's face. "Oh. Wow. That does sound nice." She'd looked away, untucking her hair from behind her ear, almost as if she was trying to hide from him. "But my life is crazy right now. I'm working two jobs and going to school. I'm surprised I even had time to come tonight." Her eyes fell on the house and her expression changed to one of longing. Liam had never regarded his childhood home with the awe and wonder she did in that moment. In many ways, the house had seemed like a prison when he was growing up. But Teresa saw it differently. He could see it on her face—she aspired to a life like the one his family had. She thought it was perfect. If only she knew the truth. "Your father has been so generous with his time and advice. I'm so thankful for his help." She turned back to him. "And I'm so glad we had a chance to meet. Perhaps we can get a drink sometime. When my life has calmed down a bit."

Liam hadn't needed more explanation than that. He'd been turned down very few times, but he knew the brush-off when he heard it. "Of course. I understand." Liam had his own craziness, working for the Christopher Corporation and trying to carve out a place for himself while living in the shadow of his dad. It would have been nice to have had a distraction as beautiful as Teresa St. Claire. Maybe even a relationship. There was a huge part of Liam that longed for a connection with a woman, in the same way Teresa seemed to long for a big, fancy house. Apparently she was *not* his dream woman. "Have a good night."

During the weeks that followed, Teresa regularly disproved her assertion that her life was too crazy for something as trivial as a dinner out. His mother had reported Teresa's regular visits to the house. She and his father were often shuttered away in his home study, and his mother, who was deeply suspicious of most people, would spend endless amounts of time speculating about what they were doing. "It's been hours, Liam. What could possibly be so important?"

If only his mother had known what torture it was for him to hear these things. He wanted Teresa, badly, and she only had time for the one man who'd never had time for him—his father. "Mom, I don't know. I'm sure it has something to do with the class she's taking."

"I think there's something else going on. I think he's having an affair with her."

That leap had made Liam sick to his stomach. His father had many personal shortcomings, but to Liam's knowledge, he'd never cheated on his mother. She'd clearly never suspected it. If she had, Liam would have heard about it. His mother told him everything. "I'm sure that's not what's going on. I'm sure it's all perfectly innocent." Only Liam wasn't so sure anymore, either. This all seemed so peculiar.

Then one night, his mother had called, frantic.

"She's here again. I can't take it, darling. I just can't do it. Your father is throwing this affair in my face."

"Mom, he's not having an affair." Liam had said it with zero conviction.

"Please come to the house. I want you to see them together. I need to know that you really believe that. If you tell me there's nothing going on, I'll believe you. You're so good at reading people. Much better than me."

The idea of seeing Teresa again brought up a complicated mix of emotions. Liam was still hurt by her declining his dinner invitation. His ego wouldn't have been so bruised if she wasn't spending a great deal of time with his dad. "It's late and I have a big day tomorrow."

"Exactly, Liam. It's late. Why would she still be here? Please come over and tell me I'm not crazy. I can hear music and laughing."

Liam's heart was filled with dread, but he couldn't say no to his mother. Her paranoid tendencies were purely a product of his father's detachment. "Okay. I can be there in thirty minutes." He'd hopped in the car and raced over, hoping to hell Teresa would just be gone by the time he arrived. Unfortunately, he was not so lucky.

"They're still in the study," his mother muttered when Liam reached the door. Her breath smelled of vodka. "The door is open a tiny bit. Will you look and see what they're doing?"

Liam had no patience for this cloak-and-dagger

routine. If the door was cracked, nothing was going on. His dad might be foolish, but he wasn't stupid. "I'm putting an end to this right now." Liam marched down the hall and raised his hand to knock on the door frame. But then he caught a glimpse of Teresa through the narrow sliver of open door. She was sitting on the edge of his father's desk, her legs crossed, a tight black skirt riding up to nearly midthigh. His father brought her a drink. Teresa toasted his father, saying she was so glad she'd found him. They smiled at each other with such adoration that Liam felt sick. They clinked their glasses and each took a sip, then Teresa hopped off the desk, gripped Linus's shoulders and kissed him tenderly on the cheek.

Liam couldn't watch anymore. He slunk away without saying a thing.

"Well?" his mother asked, waiting in the foyer.

"It's nothing." Liam hated to lie to his mother, but he needed time to think. He knew how she would react if he confirmed her suspicions. There would be chaos. And Liam couldn't afford that with his dad at that time. He was about to propose the company undertake a risky project that would eventually become the Sasha technology. He needed his dad on his side. "They're talking about stuff for his class. She must need some extra help."

"You're sure?"

Liam nodded, telling himself that he would find a way to confront his dad about Teresa. As soon as the

Sasha project was approved. "I'm sure." He'd leaned down and kissed his mom on the cheek. "Get some sleep. I'll talk to you soon."

Seven years later, that night was still so vivid in Liam's memory, and having seen Teresa only brought up the disappointment he'd had with himself over not telling his mom the truth. He walked up to The Opulence's bar and flagged the bartender. Early afternoon, and it was quiet, with just a couple sitting at one of the tables. "Club soda with lime, please." He craved something harder, but that would have to wait. He and Matt needed to have a long talk about Teresa.

"Coming up," the bartender said.

Liam took a seat at the bar. Dark thoughts and questions continued to tumble around in his head. And then it dawned on him—if Matt was so eager to give Teresa St. Claire a free pass simply because she'd worked for weeks on planning the retreat, maybe Liam needed to do some digging into her life. After all, Liam knew very little about her, and where there was one misdeed, there were often many. Maybe Liam needed to give Matt more reason to fire her.

Three

Teresa took solace in one fact—today could not get any worse. Between the threatening phone call about Joshua and running into an inexplicably irate Liam Christopher, she couldn't have imagined a more miserable beginning to her twenty-four hours at The Opulence.

"Let's get started." Matt clapped his hands. "I have a million things to get to today." He took a seat at the conference table, leaning back in the black leather chair. Despite being one of the most powerful and wealthiest men in the business world, Matt wore dark jeans and a charcoal-gray dress shirt with the sleeves rolled up. He was famous for rarely wearing a suit.

"Yes. Let's." Teresa sat opposite Matt. She pulled out her binder, already bulging with papers and notes. Matt had brought nothing but himself to the meeting, but she was used to that by now. Matt Richmond kept everything in his head. "Shall we start from the top? The guest arrival on Friday afternoon?"

Matt's blue eyes lit up. This event clearly meant a lot to him and he was excited by the prospect of knocking people's socks off. "Yes. Perfect."

Teresa began to brief Matt on the latest details. She showed off artist's renderings of the decor for The Opulence's lobby and samples of the custom room keys being printed for the weekend. She went over each item in the goody bags guests would receive, which included complimentary personalized luxury skin-care products, a $12,000 Tiffany & Co. watch with a custom cobalt blue face, and a seven-day stay at the all-new Kapalua Lanai Resort in Hawaii, the latest in Richmond Industries' hotel-management portfolio.

Matt was sparing no expense since it was his company's fifth anniversary, nor was he holding back his opinions. His reactions were mostly enthusiastic, but even the elements he was wowed by still required changes to please him. Teresa nodded and made endless notes, realizing it would be a miracle if she got any sleep at all before the retreat. There was a lot to be settled and Matt expected nothing short of perfection, and that meant she had to be perfect, too. But there were outside forces in the mix—the mystery

man, the Joshua problem and Liam. If any of them
blew up in her face before the retreat, she was sunk.

"I'd like you to go over the Saturday night gala
menu with Nadia and Aspen. Nadia knows the dietary restrictions of our VIP guests and Aspen
should be apprised of all catering decisions." Aspen
Wright was the events manager for The Opulence,
but Matt had pushed her aside in favor of Teresa.
This had already created friction.

"Nadia and I have a meeting scheduled for 3:00 p.m.
Aspen is away from the hotel today, but I'll make
sure she knows everything." Teresa had met Nadia
a few times, and they'd communicated about the retreat, but their working relationship would intensify
over the coming weeks. Teresa hoped it could be a
good one.

"Great. You two can have your meeting while
Liam and I go over the details of Saturday morning.
As soon as we've decided on everything, I'll bring
you in." When Matt had first hired Teresa, he'd asked
her to block out one hour of the retreat schedule Saturday morning for an undisclosed event.

"Liam is involved with the top-secret project?"

Matt nodded. "Something we've been working on
for years. We're keeping a very tight lid on it. He'll
be running the presentation, but I won't be able to
give you details until a day or two before the retreat.
Sorry. It's just the way it has to be."

"Of course." This made Teresa all kinds of nervous, not only because she needed to know her role

in this mysterious announcement, but also because the topic of her would invariably come up in Matt's meeting with Liam. She had to speak to Liam today, privately, to find out what he'd meant when he said that she ruined his father's life. Linus had been nothing but a fabulous mentor to her and she'd always shown her deep appreciation. He was the reason she got her start in event planning at MSM. He'd made the call to get her the interview with Mariella Santiago-Marshall. That was a professional leap that would have taken an average person years to make. It wouldn't have been possible without Linus Christopher's help.

"Are you okay?" Matt asked. "You seem distracted."

Teresa was mortified that she'd let her mind wander. "I'm perfectly fine."

Matt sat forward and smoothed his hand over the glossy wood table. "Do you want to tell me how you know Liam?"

"We met a long time ago. His father was one of my professors. It doesn't go beyond that."

"Liam seems to think it does."

Teresa drew a cleansing breath in through her nose. "I honestly have no idea what he was alluding to. Whatever it is has no bearing on my ability to plan your party."

Matt leaned back again and folded his hands over his stomach. "It seems to be affecting your concentration."

"Not at all. If I seem deep in thought, it's only because your comments gave me some ideas I'm eager to start on."

"I can't afford a single misstep, Ms. St. Claire. One whiff of trouble and I'll bring Aspen in to co-ordinate. She was unhappy with me for giving you the job."

"There won't be any problems. I can promise you that." She was used to demanding clients by now. She'd dealt with tons of them while working for MSM. The betrothal of Delilah Rhode and Alex Dane certainly stood out as a bad one. Between the happy couple's parents warring over glitz and over-the-top decadence vs. understated elegance, and the pre-wedding party that ended with the mother of the bride duking it out with Mariella Santiago-Marshall's sister over a handbag, Teresa had seen it all on that one day alone.

She'd thought coming back to Seattle would be easier, or at the very least, calmer. But now she had two very different ghosts from her past staring her down. Either could be her undoing. "Is there any-thing else, Mr. Richmond?"

"I think it's all well in hand for now. Liam should be heading in any minute. What do I say when he asks me what you said about your past?"

Teresa hated that this was still being discussed and she was eager to put an end to it. "I'm happy to stay for that part of the conversation. As I said ear-lier, I have no idea what he's talking about."

Matt shook his head. "It's okay. I'd rather skip any fireworks today. I have enough of that going on already. Let's just make sure you and Liam are ready to play nice by the time this retreat comes along."

The notion of playing nice with Liam nearly made her laugh. Oh, she'd like to play with Liam if he could drop the attitude and get back to being the sexy, brooding guy she quite enjoyed looking at. Unfortunately, she was certain he had no interest in her. "I'm always ready to play nice. As for Liam, I'm not quite sure what it will take to make him happy."

Liam filed into the meeting room minutes after Teresa left, but as near as Matt could tell, those two had not had a run-in. Liam seemed remarkably calm as he closed the door behind him. "I saw the *TBG* story." He rounded to the other side of the conference table and took a seat. "I don't want to be a jerk, but what in the hell are you doing? Sleeping with your assistant?"

A frustrated grumble left Matt's throat. He wasn't sure what to be more angry about—the fact that he'd made a mistake, the fact that the entire world knew about it or the fact that Shayla, a woman he paid an exorbitant amount of money to, had failed to do her job and get the story taken down from the site. "It just happened. We were at the hospital fund-raiser I'd had a brutal day at work, the champagne was going down a little too easy, and Nadia…"

Matt was struck with a powerful image of Nadia

in the dress she'd worn—it hugged her full hips and dipped low in the front, the gentle swell of her breasts driving him crazy. Every man in the room had noticed—a normal occurrence, as Nadia was a singular beauty—but last night it was like she was lit from within. She could have gone home with any number of men—at least a dozen asked her to dance. But she dismissed them all and stayed by Matt's side, making him laugh more than once and charming him with every flash of her eyes. Sure, he was her boss, but this had been a social affair. She wasn't obligated to do anything but have fun. It had taken only one trip around the dance floor, his hand settled on the small of her back and hers on his shoulder, their bodies pressed together, before she asked the question, "Do you want to get out of here?"

Liam waved his hand in front of Matt's face. "You were saying? Nadia?"

Matt needed to get his head out of the clouds. It wasn't like him to let a woman have this kind of effect on him. "Nadia just has this way of picking up on what I'm thinking. She got me out of my bad mood." Had she ever, although a few orgasms would do that to a guy. "Nobody else seems to care."

"I care. I just don't need to sleep with you to prove it."

"Very funny."

"I hope you're being careful. You don't have the best track record with women."

Liam wasn't wrong. Matt had a bad knack for

short-lived relationships and sleeping with women with hidden agendas. His business, his personal fortune and his family made everything more complicated. His parents were always expressing their disapproval of his romantic life. "Just settle down" was a familiar refrain. "I know. I know."

"Don't dismiss it like that. This retreat means as much to me as it does to you. I need the Sasha project to be a slam dunk. Is this really a good time for you to be in the tabloids?"

"Look. I'm on it. Shayla is killing the story."

"It doesn't matter. It's already out there."

Matt's appreciation of Liam's honesty was losing its luster. "What about you and Teresa? Is your issue with her going to become a problem? I can't pull another talented event planner out of my back pocket."

Liam's nostrils flared. That was never a good sign. Matt knew Liam well enough to recognize just how angry he was. "Did she tell you what she did? Did she own up to it?"

"No. She has no idea why you're so angry with her. And frankly, it has me wondering what is going on with you." Was the stress of Sasha getting to his best friend? Was it clouding his judgment?

"She had an affair with my dad when she was his student. That was the final straw for my mom. Teresa St. Claire is the reason she and my dad got a divorce."

"What? Seriously?"

Liam nodded solemnly. His relationship with his parents was complicated. His mother was a ball of anxiety and his father was notoriously detached. Like so many type A moguls, Linus Christopher was so focused on the bottom line that his family was of little consequence. "We both know my dad can be an idiot when it comes to interpersonal relationships, but as far as I know, he'd never cheated on my mom until Teresa came along. The fact that she's pretending as if it doesn't exist makes it so much worse."

"Are you positive they had an affair? Are you sure this isn't a case of your mom overreacting?"

"I know what you're saying, but I saw it with my own two eyes. They were in each other's arms in his office."

Matt could hardly believe what he was hearing. He didn't know Teresa particularly well, but nothing about her suggested she'd behave in such a manner. "You two need to talk this out. It was a long time ago and maybe it's time to bury the hatchet. Neither you nor I want a single thing to go wrong with this retreat. The Sasha announcement is hugely important to us both. Teresa does a top-notch job and more than anything, there's no time to find someone else. I really think you need to hash this out."

Liam pressed his lips together firmly. His mind was always going. It was one of the things Matt really admired about his best friend. No stone went unturned. But he also knew it was Liam's undoing. Overthinking never helped anything. "Fine. I'll talk to her. But I'm not promising a thing."

Four

Teresa was relieved she'd made it out of her meeting with Matt without running into Liam, but she didn't like the idea of so many loose ends. She needed to get a handle on what his problem was and smooth his ruffled feathers. She could not afford to have Matt Richmond think anything less of her. But first, she needed to reach out to Joshua and figure out what in the hell was going on. The bar was quiet, so she ducked into one of the secluded nooks, opposite a modern two-sided fireplace. She dropped down into one of the sleek chocolate-brown leather chairs and dialed the number for her brother.

The phone began to ring and she sat back, crossing her legs and gnawing on the thumbnail of her free hand. She hated feeling this anxious about Joshua. She hated worrying about him so much.

"This is Josh. Leave a message."

"Hey, Josh. It's your sister calling." She debated whether she should divulge the details of the phone call from the mystery man, but she thought better of it. She didn't want to spook her brother. "I had a spare minute between a few meetings. Thought I'd check in and see how you're doing. I hope everything is good. I miss you. I love you. Call me back when you have a chance."

She ended the call and looked at her phone for a minute, willing it to ring. *Please call back. Please call back.* It didn't happen. She took note of the time. Ten minutes before she was supposed to meet with Nadia about catering and menus. She had enough time to call The Fixer, and although she didn't look forward to it, she knew she'd feel better once she'd gotten it out of the way.

An attractive man wandered over and sat down a few yards away from her, near the tall windows that showed off the wooded vista and the falls. So much for her sliver of privacy in this part of the bar. She'd have to go outside to finish her errand.

But first a stop for a shot of liquid courage. "Bourbon. Up. Please."

The bartender nodded, flipped a glass over in one swift motion, slid it onto the bar and poured her drink. "Would you like to put this on your room?"

"Yes. I don't know the number yet, though. I arrived and walked right into a meeting."

"Don't worry. I'll find it."

Teresa took the glass in her hand and swirled the bourbon. It wasn't like her to drink during the day. It certainly was out of character with a meeting a few minutes away. But today had already been harrowing and she wasn't sure she'd make it if she didn't find a way to unwind. She tossed back the bourbon, the rush burning all the way down, followed quickly by a wave of warmth. "Thank you," she said to the bartender. She hustled back through the lobby and outside near the valet stand. She would've gone onto the patio off the bar, but the roar of the falls would've been too much. She fished her phone out of her pocket and looked up the number for The Fixer, which she didn't dare keep in her main directory. This was in a password-protected file. Her fingers trembled as she pressed the green button to make the call.

"Ms. St. Claire," The Fixer answered, his voice rich and calm. Teresa had never understood how the man could stay on such an even keel. He did terrible things, mopping up scandals and covering up lies. He made people disappear if necessary. "I wasn't expecting to hear from you."

"It's my brother. Joshua. I got a call from a man today saying Josh is in trouble again and owes seven million dollars."

"I see. And what would you like me to do about it?"

She nearly asked if the line had broken up while

she was talking. Seven million dollars and he hadn't missed a beat. "I'd like you to check on him and see if he's okay. I left him a message, but he hasn't called me back yet."

"I'm not a babysitter, Ms. St. Claire."

"I realize that. I… You know I can't be there. I'm in Seattle. I can't just hop on a plane to the east coast. My job won't allow it. Don't you have someone who can do it for me?"

"Always. I do want to remind you that I'm not a charitable organization. I do work for a fee."

However much The Fixer wanted, she was sure it would be less than seven million dollars. "Yes. Of course. Whatever you want."

"You're working for Matt Richmond right now, aren't you?"

The Fixer's ability to know everything about everyone was uncanny. And a bit terrifying. "I am."

"Keep those ties in good shape. I might need a favor."

Teresa had no idea what that could possibly mean, and the thought of owing this man anything was unsettling at best, but she wasn't about to argue. She'd worry about that down the road. "Sure. Yes."

"Okay, then. I'll have one of my associates check on Joshua's safety and look into exactly what sort of trouble he's gotten himself into."

Teresa felt so relieved, it was as if someone had removed lead weights from her shoulders. "Thank you."

"You're welcome. I do want to point out one thing, though."

"What's that?"

"Your brother is the sort of person I'm usually hired to get rid of."

A chill charged down Teresa's spine. "Excuse me?"

"He's a liability. Someone who could make a publicity nightmare. Let's be honest. That's the real reason you're calling. You don't want word to get out about your little brother. It could get you fired from working for Richmond."

How dare he make such assumptions? She might doubt herself now and then, but one thing she didn't question was whether her heart was in the right place. "You couldn't be more off base if you tried. I love him. More than anything. Just please keep him alive and out of jail."

"There's no need to get upset. I was merely connecting a few dots. I will have someone check on Joshua and I'll get back to you as soon as I can."

"Hurry. Please." Teresa hung up the phone, unable to ignore the way her heart was threatening to pound its way out of her chest. She straightened her jacket and turned, only to see Nadia, Matt's assistant, less than ten feet away, chatting with one of the doormen. Teresa stopped in place, her mind scrambled as she tried to remember the exact words she'd said to The Fixer. Had Nadia heard the conversation? So many thoughts had been zipping through Teresa's brain, it was hard to know the difference between the things she'd said and the things she'd kept to herself.

She approached Nadia. "Hey there. Are you ready to sit down and have our meeting?" Teresa clung to her forced composure. Her future and the success of her company depended on it. She'd never be able to truly help Joshua if she got fired from the biggest job of her life.

Nadia didn't let on that she'd heard every minute of Teresa's side of the phone call she'd made. "Is it okay if I pull you into an impromptu meeting with Shane Adams and Isabel Withers? Shane is the president of the Richmond Hotel Group. Isabel is The Opulence's concierge. She has some ideas for couples' activities during the retreat."

"Ooh. Couples' activities? I'm intrigued." She laughed quietly. If Teresa was in any way upset by her call, she didn't let it show.

Nadia waved her inside. "Come on. I'll introduce you. Shane is only here for a few more minutes, and I need to catch him. He's one of those people who's so busy it's impossible to schedule a meeting." The two strode back into the lobby. Ahead, Isabel was sitting at her desk near check-in while Shane was standing a few feet away, his nose in his phone. "Hi, guys. I just need to grab a few minutes of your time."

"Good." Shane darkened the screen on his phone but held on to it like it was his lifeline. "I have a crazy schedule today."

Nadia didn't bother acknowledging his statement. Shane was a workaholic. Everyone knew it and there was no use telling the guy to slow down and breathe. "I wanted to see how we can bring Isabel in on the retreat. Since she's started working here, the resort has really gained a reputation as a romantic destination."

Isabel smiled and stood proud. Her red hair was up in a polished twist, but a few strands framing her face softened her usually austere styling. "Actually, I like to refer to myself as a romance—"

Shane's phone rang loudly. He glanced at the screen and muted it. "Sorry. I'll call them back in a minute."

Isabel cleared her throat and tried again. "Well, let's just say that I like to play up our more romantic amenities, and Nadia had mentioned that so many of the guests are coming with a spouse or significant other. The spa is available for couples' massages. We can have Housekeeping put out candles at night and turn down the bed with rose petals. There are romantic dinners, of course, and couples' yoga. Really whatever people want."

"Perhaps it would be best if we present our guests with a menu of services prior to their arrival," Teresa offered.

"I can call them a week before the retreat and find out exactly what they want," Isabel said.

"That sounds great," Nadia said.

Shane looked a bit lost. "I guess my only concern

is whether we have enough staff to handle these requests."

"I have a list of massage therapists and other local vendors if we need to bring in additional help," Isabel said. "I think it could be a real boon if we get some celebrities and A-listers talking about what we offer here."

"Yes. The feedback we've received on your job performance has been quite positive," Shane said.

Isabel's face flushed bright pink. "Thank you," she said.

Nadia couldn't help but notice the whiff of romance in the air and not just because Isabel was focused on creating it. The way she looked at Shane, with both adoration and longing, made Nadia wonder if that was her expression when her gaze fell on Matt. Perhaps she'd been too hard on him earlier. Of course, they had to stop this runaway train, but she should probably stop throwing around words like *mistake*. "It sounds like we're all on the same page. Teresa and Isabel, if you can coordinate and let me know if you need any help, that would be great."

"Are we done?" Shane asked. "Sorry, I really need to go."

Isabel's face fell, telling Nadia her suspicions were correct. There was a major crush happening here and it was all traveling in one direction.

"Yes. Thanks." Nadia turned to Teresa. "Is it all right if we go upstairs and meet in Matt's suite? My laptop is up there."

"Sure," Teresa said.

The two women made their way upstairs, settling in the most suitable work area in Matt's room, at the dining table near the writing desk. They went over the menus for the entire weekend and came up with a long list of questions for Aspen. Accommodating each guest's dietary guidelines would be a challenge, but Nadia felt as though she'd successfully handed the baton to Teresa.

"Any other questions?" Nadia asked.

Teresa shook her head. "I don't think so."

"Everything else is going well? No bumps in the road?" Nadia stopped short of asking about Teresa's phone conversation. She hoped she might explain it on her own. If she didn't, Nadia had to mention it to Matt.

"I need to sort out a few things with Liam Christopher, but otherwise, no."

"I could see how there might be issues. The Sasha announcement is going to be big. Both Matt and Liam are pretty anxious about it. Liam's been working on this technology for years."

Teresa cocked her head as if Nadia had taken her by surprise. "So that's what it's called? Sasha?"

Nadia felt the blood drain from her face. "Did Matt not tell you in your meeting? I thought he was telling you today."

She shook her head. "He said he wanted to keep a lid on it a little longer. I guess Liam is paranoid about the news getting out."

Nadia closed her eyes and pinched the bridge of her nose. "You can't breathe a word of this to anyone. I need you to promise me you won't. Matt and Liam will never forgive me."

"Of course." Teresa raised a finger to her lips. "Your secret's safe with me."

Nadia wasn't sure she could trust Teresa. She needed to give herself a little insurance. And the only ammunition she had was the information she'd gained an hour ago. "I hope your phone call downstairs wasn't anything too important. I'm sorry, but I couldn't help but overhear."

Teresa blanched, her skin pale as a ghost. "That was personal and I'd like to keep it that way. Surely you understand. Just like you wouldn't want me talking about the *TBG* story."

Nadia swallowed hard. Teresa was not afraid to throw a punch when needed. "That was taken down from the website right before our meeting. There's nothing to talk about anymore."

Teresa gathered her things. "Here's some free advice. Women are judged for these things far more harshly than men. The world is changing, but we aren't there yet. You need to protect yourself. Put your own interests first. You know Matt Richmond won't hesitate to do the same."

Nadia knew Teresa was right. Nadia had given herself virtually that exact speech in the car on her way up to The Opulence. "I hope I can trust you to keep the story to yourself."

"Of course. Bad tabloid news is the last thing I want interfering with this event." Teresa got up from the table while Nadia tried to ignore the way her statement made her stomach sour. "I'm going to my room to get freshened up before I head into my last meeting today."

Nadia showed Teresa to the door. When she glanced down the hall, she saw Matt striding toward them. Her heart made its presence known, thumping wildly.

"Mr. Richmond," Teresa said.

Matt's sights flashed to Nadia for an instant, making heat rush through her. "Please. Call me Matt. The next month and a half is going to be crazy. We might as well get to a first-name basis now."

"Great. Thank you very much for today. And don't hesitate to reach out any time, day or night, if you need anything at all." She started to walk away, but Matt stopped her.

"You can start by making peace with Liam. You two have some things to work out and I'd like it taken care of before you head back to Seattle tomorrow morning."

"Certainly. I'll track him down," she responded, then continued down the hall.

Nadia couldn't help but wonder what that exchange had been about, but she needed to focus on controlling herself. Her desire to take off Matt's shirt right now was overwhelming. She couldn't stop looking at the buttons of his shirt, her fingers twitching at the thought. "I heard the *TBG* story went away," she said quietly.

He nodded and placed his hand on her back, sending waves of warmth though her. "Come inside. This isn't a conversation for the hallway."

Nadia froze for a moment, knowing exactly how she was going to feel the minute they were alone.

"It's okay, Nadia. I won't bite."

She blew out a frustrated breath and breezed past him. "I know that."

As soon as the door was closed, he took her hand. "That is unless you want me to."

Five

Here they were, all alone, no one to bother them. "Matt, I'm sorry about what I said earlier. I could have found a nicer way to say what I did. I don't want you to think I regret last night."

"You sure? I'd rather you just be honest with me if you're really feeling that way. I'm big on honesty. You should know that by now." His voice was a low, sexy rumble that shook Nadia to her core.

"I do not regret it. Scout's honor."

"Good. I would hate that." He stretched his arms above his head and yawned, his biceps straining against his shirtsleeves. It was one of the sexiest things a man had ever done in her presence.

"You tired?" she asked.

"Exhausted. Somebody kept me up until four thirty in the morning." His eyebrows bobbed up and down.

"And it nearly ended up being an international incident."

He shrugged. "I've seen worse. And even better, it's gone now. No one from the office has said anything to you, have they?"

Teresa wasn't really a coworker, so she let it go and shook her head. "No. Crisis averted, I guess."

"So that's that, then. We go back to the way things were before. We don't say anything about it. We pretend like it doesn't exist?"

All she could think about was that she didn't want to go back to the way things were before. She didn't want to pretend like it hadn't happened, even when she knew that was the sensible thing to do. "I'm worried I haven't fully gotten you out of my system."

He grinned and walked across the room, then poured them each a drink. "You already know I haven't gotten you out of mine. I told you as much earlier." He turned and handed her a glass, clinking his with hers. "Here's to a woman with all the power."

Nadia took a sip for courage, wondering if that was really true. Could she have a man like Matt at her beck and call? Was it as simple as telling him she wanted him? Her heart was beating so fiercely at the prospect that it was threatening to march its way outside of her body. "So I'm calling the shots here?"

"Whatever you want." He took a sip of his drink, but he didn't take his eyes off her. When he set his glass back on the table, he stepped closer. "We're all alone."

Everything about him was so overwhelming—his woodsy cologne, his hair begging to be touched and her knowledge of what his chest looked like out of that shirt. "I do like that thing you do with your mouth." She bit her lower lip as soon as she'd said it. She'd never uttered anything so bold to a man, but it was freeing to be honest.

"This?" He placed the softest tease of a kiss on her lips, making her light-headed.

"That's a good start."

"Or maybe I should kiss you somewhere else." He popped the buttons of her blouse free, one by one. His determined fingers traveled lower, while want and need were the strongest forces at work in her body. He peeled back her blouse and slipped her bra strap from her shoulder. Pulling the lacy cup down from her breast, he lowered his head and drew her nipple into his mouth, gripping her rib cage with both of his firm hands.

Nadia gasped. He swirled his tongue. Her skin puckered and drew tight. She dug her fingers into his thick hair. "Both. Please. Now."

"Wait. One more."

A clever and slightly devious smile crossed his lips. He dragged his hands down her waist to her hips, dropping to his knees. He slipped his fingers under the hem of her skirt and pushed up the fabric, gathering it as he went, palms flat against her thighs. Nadia could hardly believe what was happening— one of the most brilliant and powerful men in the world was about to pleasure her. His eyes swirled darker and he tugged her black lace panties to one side, leaving her bare to him. He nestled his face between her legs, his tongue finding her apex. A jolt of electricity hit her so hard her legs nearly buckled. She reached for the back of the chair behind her, but that only gave him better access. He had her at his mercy. She would give him anything he wanted.

"Matt, please. I want it all. I want you." Even in the moment, wrapped up in the urgency of wanting him naked and the heat that was coursing between her legs, she couldn't escape the weight of her words. She wanted it all—this magnificent man *and* the amazing job that went along with him.

"Good." He rose to standing and took her hand, leading her to the bedroom while he used his free hand to untuck his shirt. They stepped inside the gloriously appointed room and Nadia took charge, turning him around with a tug on his hand. They smashed their bodies and mouths against each other. Tongues swirling. Hot and wet. Her fingers scrambled through the buttons of his shirt and she pushed the garment off his shoulders, never letting the contact of their lips break. Next were his pants, which fell to the floor. Matt stepped out and pulled on her elbows, walking backward to the bed. He sat on the corner of the mattress.

"Why are you still wearing so many clothes?"

She laughed quietly. "Because someone hasn't taken them off yet."

"It's impossible to get good help these days. Let me start with that skirt." With a twirl of his finger, he invited her to turn her back to him. He drew down the zipper, then the skirt and finally her panties, all the way to her ankles. A groan escaped his lips. She loved hearing that noise, knowing that he wanted her. "The shoes stay on," he said.

She looked back at Matt over her shoulder. His normally bright eyes were dark with desire. "Yes, sir." She bent over and carefully stepped out of the panties while Matt cupped her bottom with his hands and got an eyeful in the process. She straightened and turned in his arms, wearing only her bra and black stilettos.

Still sitting, Matt wrapped one arm around her waist and pressed soft open-mouth kisses against her belly while dragging his fingers up the inside of her thighs. Everything she had been feeling that morning was tenfold now. Her thighs weren't merely on fire. They felt like they would never cool down. He spread her folds with his fingers and pressed his thumb against her center, working in circles and making her dizzy. She reached behind and unhooked her bra, casting it aside. She raised one leg to give him better access, planting her foot on the bed. She'd never felt so sexy in her entire life. Matt slid a finger inside her, his thumb still applying the perfect amount of pressure.

"I love how wet you get for me." Matt slipped a second finger inside, slowly gliding deeper.

"Honestly? Just being around you makes me wet." It was so liberating to let go of these things she normally held so tightly in her head. She dug one hand into his hair and with the other cupped her own breast, rolling her nipple between her fingertips. The pleasure coiled between her legs. Matt had her so close.

Matt groaned again. "Seeing you touch yourself is so hot."

The pressure was becoming too much. She was having a hard time keeping her eyes open. "I'm going to come if you aren't careful."

"Just let go. I want to watch you unravel. Then I'll do it to you again."

That was all she needed. She sucked in a breath and the orgasm rolled through her, her muscles drawing tight and releasing. Again. And again. She looked down at Matt and their gazes connected, hot and intense, as the waves of pleasure continued. She lowered her head and kissed him slowly and deeply, telling him just how incredible that had been. "Your fingers are amazing, but I want to feel you inside me," she muttered against his lips. "I want you holding me down against the bed."

"That's what I want, too. I'll get a condom." Matt

sprang up from the bed and Nadia tugged back the fluffy white duvet, then took her few seconds of alone time to arrange herself seductively on the bed, lying on her side, black heels a sexy contrast to the bright white of the bedding.

When Matt reappeared, he was a vision, and a naked one at that—long legs, firm muscles and abs she wanted to outline with her tongue. He tossed her the foil packet and she tore it open as he set a knee on the mattress. She reached out and wrapped her hand around his rock-hard erection, stroking firmly and rolling her thumb over the swollen tip. Matt closed his eyes and placed his hands on his hips, jutting them forward. Nadia scooted closer on the bed and took him in her mouth, her tongue pressing against the underside of his length. She felt the tension in his pelvis. She wanted every ounce of energy he was holding back. The need was centered between her legs, but she needed him on an even more primal level, like she was hardwired to want him. Unable to wait any longer, she gently let go and rolled on the condom.

She rolled to her back and spread her legs wide for him. Matt climbed onto the bed and positioned himself between her knees. He took his length in hand and lowered himself, slowly driving inside. Inch by inch she learned all over again how perfect a fit he was. This was even more sublime than it had been last night. She was no longer wrapped up in surprise. She could enjoy it, and she did, relishing every artful rotation of his hips. She wrapped her legs around him, pulling him in closer, feeling at one with him. His strokes were deep and strong, already aiming her straight for her peak. She was so torn. She loved to look at him, but it took so much strength to keep her eyes open. She pivoted her hips to let him go even deeper. Closer. But that's when the pressure started to become too much to take. She sucked in a sharp breath and Matt's breathing grew choppy and short. He dropped to his elbows, planted them above her shoulders and burrowed his face in her neck. He kissed the sensitive skin beneath her ear, licking then nipping at her lobe. Meanwhile, he employed the most glorious rocking of his hips, which doubled the hot friction against her center. Every pass had her a little bit closer, but she wanted to wait for him. She wanted them to reach this point together.

"Are you close?" she asked.

"Mmm-hmm," he groaned. "Very."

Nadia focused on holding on, but after a few more strokes, it became too much and she gave way. That was apparently enough for Matt. He followed right behind, pulsing inside her as she felt her own body grab on to his. Everything had fallen into rhythm—breaths and heartbeats, kisses and moans. Matt pulled back his head and smoothed her hair from her face. He kissed her deeply as the final delicious swells of satisfaction rolled through her. She knew then that this was way more than sex or a mind-blowing orgasm. It was like she was rolling around on a cloud, floating up in space, light as air.

"You're amazing." He dotted her collarbone with dozens of kisses, then rolled to her side.

"You're the amazing one." She curled into him, pressing her lips against his chest and drawing in his perfectly masculine smell. She knew she shouldn't feel so content in his arms. So happy.

"I want you to stay the night. No one will have to see you sneaking out. We can be together. All night. Until morning."

She smiled, but on the inside her heart was breaking. She knew this wasn't right. They couldn't continue like this. Their day away from the office was a fantasy. As soon as reality crept back in, this connection she had with Matt would go up in smoke. "Until morning. Sounds perfect."

Matt had asked Liam to experience as much of The Opulence as he could during his brief overnight stay. Liam was nothing but a good friend, so he'd holed up in the bar, enjoying a manhattan and taking note of the ambience and amenities. There were several dozen people around, mostly couples enjoying the multitude of fireplaces and cozy places to sit, while off in the dark, Centennial Falls continued its endless churn.

Liam had found a quiet corner booth in the bartender's direct line of vision so he could signal for a refill. At the table next to his, a man and woman were kissing. Liam had never understood public displays of affection. He didn't believe in putting on a show. Still, he felt a pang of jealousy. He wished he could tune out the rest of the world like that. Get lost in a woman. Take a break from the endless cycle of work, work and more work.

He finished his drink and decided he couldn't stomach any more time spent alone while things were heating up at the next table. He was about to slide out of the booth when in walked Teresa St. Claire. He froze, unsure whether he should try to sneak out or stay put and hope she wandered off elsewhere.

And then there was a third option—sit back and admire her. She still hadn't spotted him and he would've been lying if he'd said he wasn't enjoying watching her. She'd changed clothes and was now wearing a showstopper of a dress—black, off both shoulders and hugging every curve. Her blond hair was up in a high ponytail and he could imagine how much fun it might be to tug on it. He still wasn't sure what to make of her. The few times he'd had his investigator look into someone, he'd gotten at least an initial report lightning-fast. Usually within an hour. Not with Teresa. Everything discovered so far was the stuff he already knew. *Dig deeper*, he'd told his investigator. Everyone had dirt. Everyone.

Teresa turned in his direction and caught sight of him. She wasted no time and sauntered toward him, hips in full sway. "There you are." She looked down at him, perfect eyebrows arched high, crimson lips pursed.

Liam struggled to find an appropriate response. Matt had told him to make peace. "You found me out. I'm in the bar, drinking too much."

She set her clutch handbag on the table. "Scoot over, okay?"

He did as she asked and she slid into the bench seat right next to him. Her perfume hit him first, something he hadn't noticed earlier when he'd been so angry. It was sweet and soft, everything he wasn't. "Can I get you a drink?" he asked.

"What are you having? Or I guess I should say what *were* you having?" She picked up his empty glass and rattled the ice.

"A manhattan."

"How very stodgy and old-fashioned of you." She smiled, letting him know she was only having fun.

"It's a classic."

"Fine. I'll have one, too."

Liam flagged the bartender, flashed him two fingers and pointed at his empty glass. "To what do I owe this visit? Were you seriously looking for me?"

"Matt wants us to iron out our differences and I do everything Matt says. This job is very important to me."

Just when he was starting to relax, the reality of the job before them hit hard. "He expressed the same sentiments to me. He'd like us to at least make peace." Liam still wasn't sure how he felt about the idea. He'd been holding on to ill feelings toward her for years. Her physical presence was certainly helping to soften his opinion of her, though. He could admit that much.

The waiter brought the drinks from the bar, removed Liam's empty and then moved away to give them privacy.

Teresa held up her glass to toast. "To peacemaking."

Liam wasn't convinced it was possible, but this was his third drink so he was certainly more optimistic than he'd been an hour or two ago.

Teresa stirred her drink, stabbing at the ice cubes, then sat back and looked at Liam. They were shoulder to shoulder, arms touching. He admired the exposed contours of her collarbone, the shimmer of her skin. She was stunning. On any other day, with any other woman who looked like her, Liam would have been making a concerted effort to seduce her. Not Teresa. He might be tempted but he wasn't stupid.

"So. Tell me why you hate me," she said.

"That's a question straight out of high school if ever I heard one."

"It wasn't a question, it was a directive, and I'm sorry if my getting to the point bothers you, but I'd just like to know what the hell happened today."

He pressed his lips together tightly, choking back the grumble in his throat. He needed to come out with it and find a way to get past it, at least temporarily.

"Your relationship with my father was the beginning of the end of my parents' marriage. Now neither of them is happy, especially not my dad, who had to move out of the house and is now even more of a workaholic than he used to be."

"My relationship with your dad was a two-way street. I never forced him to take me under his wing. And he approached me. I was too intimidated by him to say a thing." She took another sip. "And almost no one intimidates me."

"Take you under his wing? Is that what we're calling it? I'm not a fan of that particular spin, honestly. Let's call it what it was. An affair."

Teresa clunked her glass down on the table and shot him a look that was equal parts insulted and astonished. "An affair?" she asked, a little too loudly.

"Hold your voice. People are looking." Liam shifted in his seat. "I can't afford to have an argument with a beautiful woman in a public place. Some idiot with a camera phone will make my life a living nightmare."

"I did not have an affair with your father. That's a lie. I don't know who told you that, but it's not true."

"Nobody needed to tell me. I saw it with my own eyes." Liam took a long slug of his drink to ward off the mental images of that night, but they were coming right at him, one after another. "You two in his study. Drinking. Laughing. Toasting. Your skirt up to the middle of your thighs. And then you hop off his desk and kiss him. I can't believe you would do that, especially in the house he shared with my mother. She welcomed you into her home and that's how you treat our family?"

For a moment, Teresa did nothing more than nod and look him square in the eye. It was almost as if Liam could see the cogs turning. "Laughing and toasting? I kissed him?"

"Yes."

She shook her head emphatically. "No. That was the day I got the job with MSM Event Planning in Santa Barbara. Your dad arranged the interview with Mariella Santiago-Marshall, which was an impossible ticket to get. Every future event planner in the world wants to train with her. That's why we were toasting. That's why I kissed him. On the cheek, I might mention. I never, ever kissed your father on the mouth. It would be rude. And strange. He was my mentor."

Liam wasn't sure he should believe her. Teresa was clearly a fast thinker and, of course, anyone who was trying to save their current job could fabricate a story to explain their past misdeeds. "You realize I don't have any reason to believe you. I saw what I saw."

"No, you saw something that was purely innocent. I swear. Me being mystified at your attitude toward me earlier today was genuine. Now you know why I had no idea why you were angry. Honestly, I thought it was because I turned you down, which seemed a little absurd since it was seven years ago and…" She turned and eyed him up and down. "Look at you. You can have any woman you want."

Liam could admit that he had been hurt by the way she'd dismissed him all those years ago, but perhaps that was because she was the only woman who'd captured his imagination in no time at all. "Now you're trying to deflect."

"I'm not. You're easily one of Seattle's top five most eligible bachelors. I'm sure your bed is plenty busy."

"That's an awfully big assumption."

"No, it's not. I know men. When anything is theirs for the taking, they take."

If only it was that easy. Liam had never had a relationship that lasted longer than a few weeks. It was simply too difficult for him to be at ease with someone. To trust. He found himself questioning everything and everyone. "My tastes are discerning. I won't fall for just a pretty face."

"Of course not. I'm sure you want the whole package. Long legs, great boobs, beautiful hair."

Like you, Liam nearly said. "I'm not opposed if that's what you're asking."

Teresa knocked her knee into his leg. "I'll keep that in mind. This single girl doesn't want to stay that way forever. For now, I want us to get along. Frankly, I need us to get along if I'm going to be helping you with the announcement of this big secret project of yours."

Liam drew in a deep breath. Perhaps Teresa was

right. Perhaps Matt was, too. With his private investigator on the case, Liam would discover the dirt on Teresa St. Claire. He didn't have to take her word for it. And in the meantime, that one-hour time slot on Saturday morning during the retreat was immensely important to him. He needed to wave the white flag of surrender, at least for the moment. "Fine. We will declare a cease-fire."

"Not a truce?"

He shook his head. "I'm not sure I trust you enough for that."

Teresa stirred her drink again then looked over at him, their gazes connecting. Liam felt as though she was drawing electricity from thin air and sending it right through him. "Then we're even. Because I don't trust you, either."

Six

Nadia had been back in the office for a little more than a day after her tryst with Matt at The Opulence. It had been a lonely return, and not just because it was the inevitable crash back to reality. Matt had a business emergency in Miami and had left straight from the resort that next morning. They'd made love before he left, just a quickie, but it had been truly bittersweet. She'd had no choice but to remind him afterward that it couldn't happen again. He'd only said that he understood before leaving her with a parting kiss that lingered on her lips for hours.

Matt was set to return today and that left Nadia a jumble of emotions. She was always excited to see him, but she was also quite certain that people in the office were talking about them. Those not-so-discreet whispers would likely become harder to detect when he was back, but Nadia was certain they'd continue until she and Matt gave the office busybodies something else to talk about.

She was finishing up an email when her phone beeped with a text. She turned and glanced at the screen, seeing a name she hadn't thought about in quite some time—Hideo Silva. She and Hideo had been close friends in high school but hadn't seen or spoken to each other in at least four years.

In Seattle today for a photo shoot. Would love to grab a drink. I miss you!

Hideo was a top-tier male model, traveling the world, appearing in countless magazines and regularly dating Hollywood starlets. It was part of the reason he and Nadia rarely spoke. He was off living a jet-set life she couldn't keep up with. I have a party to go to for work. Do you want to come with me? I miss you, too!

I would love it. Can't wait to catch up. I'll call at 6 and we'll make a plan for me to pick you up?

Perfect. See you then!

Nadia returned her phone to her desk, wondering how Matt would react to this development. There was nothing romantic between herself and Hideo, and there never would be. But he was devastatingly handsome and most men did not react well to being around him. Nadia had witnessed it dozens of times in high school. But perhaps the timing of Hideo's visit was perfect. She and Matt needed to get back on a more professional track. As amazing as their night at The Opulence had been, it was a startling example of how little self-control she had when it came to him. She'd gone there determined to end it and she'd done exactly the opposite. Even worse, her resolve had lasted only a few hours before they ended up in bed together again. She'd told herself "one more time," but that wasn't the way it had happened at all. They'd spent all night making love. They ordered dinner in. Nadia hadn't spent more than a minute in her own room.

Out of the corner of her eye, Nadia spotted Shayla, the head of PR, marching down the wide corridor outside Matt's office. On the surface, Shayla was drop-dead gorgeous, with long silky black hair and a flawless complexion. Her tastes were discerning and expensive. Only the finest designer clothing, shoes and accessories would do. But once you knew the real Shayla, it cast her assets in a distinctly different light. She was ruthless. She scared the crap out of the interns in the office, and most of the admins for that matter. With a single pointed glare, she could send a person running to the bathroom in tears. But Shayla was excellent at her job, one of the best in the world. She was also one of Matt's original employees, and thus afforded herself all of the snobbery that she could claim from having been around longer than anyone else.

"If it isn't the beauty queen," Shayla quipped.

"Please don't call me that. I know you don't mean it as a compliment."

"Fine then, Ms. Gonzalez. We need to have a chat about a few things." Shayla wrinkled her nose. "Things I'd rather not bring up with HR."

Nadia felt like the bottom of her stomach fell out. She fought back her inclination to bark at Shayla that HR ultimately took orders from Matt, and Matt was not going to let Nadia get in trouble. But she wasn't entirely sure that was true. She'd only known Matt for fourteen months and she'd spent every minute of that time with a monster crush on him. She'd seen sweet, affable Matt Richmond throw very good people under the bus. "Okay. Shoot."

Shayla perched herself on the edge of Nadia's desk and took a long gander in both directions before speaking. Shayla never wanted anyone to catch her saying something horrible, and she'd said plenty of ugly things to Nadia. "I'd like to get the lay of the land here, just so I can be prepared to deal with it if the press comes to me. Did you start sleeping with our boss right away or did you spend a few months wagging that curvy bum of yours in his face before he had a weak moment?" Shayla admired her manicure as if she'd asked Nadia the most innocuous of questions.

Nadia felt her whole body get cold. "This was a recent thing."

Shayla nodded, but there was so much snide skepticism on her face Nadia wondered how she could hold her head up straight. "Recent like a month ago? Right before he gave you that new car as a bonus?"

Nadia was horrified at Shayla's suggestion, but she knew very well that it could be misconstrued that way. "That was for a job well done. I worked hard for that car."

Shayla raised an eyebrow. "I bet."

Nadia wasn't going to have this conversation. Shayla had shown her cards too soon. "Can I help you with something? I have work to do."

"No. Just wanted to let you know that I don't appreciate having to clean up your messes. Or even worse, having to take the heat for it. If you're going to carry on like this, at least take the time to be discreet. You didn't bother to stay in your own room at The Opulence? How obvious can you be?"

"That's not true. I had my own room."

"Nobody slept in your bed."

"You don't know that."

"Oh, but I do. I have connections everywhere in this company. From the highest executives all the way down to Housekeeping at our management properties."

Nadia was really going to have to watch her back. There was no telling how much gossiping Shayla might do. She was tight with a lot of people in the company. "I'd prefer it if you didn't devote so much time to digging up dirt on me."

"Don't tell me what to do with my time. You are on very thin ice here. You're already past your expiration date with Matt."

"Expiration date?"

"You've worked here for fourteen months. He's never kept an admin for longer than a year. I think he gets tired of the scenery. Wants a change of pace."

"He's not like that."

"Oh, no? Matt is an unimaginably wealthy, powerful and handsome guy. He can have any woman in the world. You think you're so special because you won a beauty pageant when you were a teenager? That was a long time ago."

"I have my job because I'm good at it. And that's the reason I've kept it, too."

"Then I suggest you focus on that. You can start with that party Gideon Johns is hosting tonight. I know you and Matt are both going to be there. Maybe try not to play footsie with Mr. Richmond while you're there."

"For your information, I'm bringing a date."

From down the hall Nadia could hear a chorus of voices saying, "Good morning, Mr. Richmond."

Shayla hopped off Nadia's desk. "We didn't have this conversation."

Nadia didn't bother to reply. Anything she said would be turned against her.

Matt strolled up to them, all smiles. As serious and hard-nosed as he could be, Matt was always warm and pleasant with her. He made her heart melt a little bit every time she saw him. "Ladies," he said. "Are we having a meeting of the minds this morning?"

"Nadia and I were talking about Gideon Johns's party tonight. Should be fun."

"Oh. Right. I forgot about that."

"I'll see you both later this evening," Shayla said, slinking back into whatever hole she'd climbed out of.

Nadia rose from her desk and took Matt's jacket from him. "Party starts at seven. No dinner, just heavy hors d'oeuvres. Mr. Johns booked one of his favorite bands."

"Of course he did. The guy is a music junkie." Matt took several strides into his office, but stopped and turned back. "You coming?"

Nadia was stuck, frozen, unsure what to do. This was the first time they'd been together in the office since sleeping together. She normally wouldn't think twice about following him into his office. Now she was worried about who was watching and what sorts of signals she might be putting off. The fact that the walls of his office were entirely made of glass wasn't helping the situation. The instant someone lowered the privacy shades, everyone would start to gossip. She knew very well how the rumor mill worked. "Of course." She crossed the threshold and closed the door behind them. People might be able to see, but she didn't want them to be able to hear.

Matt got situated behind his desk, taking out his laptop and plugging in his phone to charge. "Have you heard from Liam by any chance? I've been trying to reach him, but I just get his voice mail. I want him to rethink coming to Gideon's party tonight. I think he'd have fun."

"I'm not sure, but I can certainly try to get him on the phone."

"Thanks."

Nadia took a step closer to his desk, feeling awkward and intimidated. "Matt, I hate to bring up personal stuff at work, but I just want to make sure we're both on the same page with what happened at The Opulence."

He nodded, sat back in his chair and folded his hands across his stomach, bringing to mind the feel of his muscled abs beneath her hands. Damn, she was going to miss that. "We agreed it was the last time, right? I mean it's a real shame, but I get it. We should just be glad that tabloid story didn't blow up in our faces."

"That's what I wanted to talk about. It sort of has. At least for me. People are whispering when I walk by and one person actually said something to me about it."

Matt raised both eyebrows, creating those adorable crinkles in his forehead. "What happened?"

Nadia didn't want to get too specific. There was no divulging Shayla as the source without it later coming back to haunt her. "Let's just say that I got a few snide comments about sleeping with the boss. And an assumption that it might be tied to the car you gave me as a bonus."

He shook his head. "No. You earned that car. Fair and square. That was a good month before anything happened."

"I know that. You know that. But you can also imagine how it looks. I can't afford for anyone at work to see me in a light that's less than professional. I need this job. It's important to me."

"I'm not going to fire you. You're the best admin I've ever had, by far."

"And you know that it isn't just your decision. All sorts of outside forces can come into play if a particularly bad story gets out. The board of directors. Stockholders. You have to answer to people, Matt. You aren't an autonomous ruler."

His lips pressed into a thin line. She hated that look of concern on his face. It didn't suit him. "Don't remind me."

"I'm just saying that for both of our sakes, we should agree that we had fun together, but now we're back to the way things were before."

He blew out a breath and took a glance out the window. "Agreed. I don't like it, but I agree."

She wasn't sure what about it he didn't like—the idea of not getting to have sex with her anymore? But she wasn't going to press for additional information. She had what she wanted. "Great. I'm glad we agree."

He turned back in his chair. "When you say you need this job, do you mean you really need it? Like things would get bad if you lost it?"

Nadia nearly laughed. Matt was very down-to-earth, but he'd grown up with extraordinary wealth. The man had never wanted for anything. "Yes. Things would get bad. I need to earn a living, Matt. Just like almost everyone."

"What kind of bad? Because if we aren't paying you enough, I can fix that."

"This is not the time to give me a raise."

"You didn't answer my question, though. What kind of bad?"

Nadia didn't like to talk about her personal life at work, but she couldn't deny that she and Matt had a strong connection. He was sweet and caring. He was interested in people's lives. "My parents rely on me to help make ends meet. My mom got sick right before I came to work here. Breast cancer. She's okay, but my parents didn't have great insurance. My mom is a teacher and my dad owns a coffee-roasting business and a handful of coffee shops. Money was always tight. So, I stepped in to help, just so they wouldn't have to risk losing their home. That house is a big piece of their retirement. I wasn't willing to let them lose that."

"I had no idea. Why didn't you tell me this before?"

Nadia shrugged, feeling a bit embarrassed. "Because it had nothing to do with my job. I mean, lots of people have burdens. I'm helping my parents pay off some medical bills. I'm helping with my sister's college tuition. It's not a big deal. I have a budget and I stick to it and it's not a problem. I'm not wanting for anything."

"But if you lost your job, all of that would fall apart."

"Well, yeah."

He nodded solemnly. "Okay. I get it. We can't allow ourselves to get into a situation where any doubt could be cast on your abilities. We'll focus on work and leave what happened in the past."

Matt had just said everything she'd wanted him to say. This was the smart course and Nadia prided herself on being sensible. So why was she feeling so profoundly sad? "Just a memory."

"An incredibly hot one."

Nadia shook her head. Matt was going to be the death of her. "Do you need anything right now? If not, I'm going to get back to my desk."

"No. I'm good."

Nadia headed for the door.

"Oh, uh, Nadia. You're coming to Gideon's party

tonight, right? Do you need a ride? I can have my car come by and scoop you up."

She smiled sweetly while digging her fingernails into the heels of her hands. "I am going, but I don't need a ride. I'm actually bringing a date." The instant the words left her lips, she felt a deep urge to explain herself. She didn't want to hurt Matt, no matter what. But she also had to be strong for once. If she had a means of putting up walls with him, she should do it. It would be better for both of them in the long run.

"I see. Someone special?"

"An old friend. Hideo Silva. He lives in New York, but he's in town for work."

"What does he do for a living?"

"He's a male model."

Matt averted his eyes and gathered some papers on his desk. "Excellent. Well, have fun."

"It's not a big deal. We're just friends." The words came out a bit desperate and Nadia hated that she'd bothered to divulge this information.

He popped his eyebrows at her and nodded. "It's a free country, Nadia. I have no control over you."

"I didn't want you to think…"

"What? That you'd moved on? We had our fun, Nadia. You made it clear that it's not going to happen again."

Nadia nodded solemnly, but all the while her stomach soured and her heart felt as though it was crumbling. "I guess I'd better get back to my desk."

"Yes. I think that's for the best."

* * *

Teresa was glad she had Gideon Johns's party to-night to distract her. Not that she wasn't incredibly busy. She'd never worked harder or slept less, but she had it under control, and most important, Te-resa always worked best under pressure. Plus, all of this preoccupation was keeping her mind off Liam.

She couldn't get that conversation in the bar off her mind. He had looked good enough to kiss, and under any other circumstance, she would have tried her hardest to persuade him that was a great idea. She would have done everything in her power to take Liam upstairs to her room at The Opulence. But because of what he thought of her—that she'd had an affair with his father and ruined his parents' marriage—well, she couldn't risk him thinking she was a woman with a big arsenal of feminine wiles. She certainly couldn't flirt. Liam was hands-off. At least until the retreat was over.

Luckily, although Liam had been invited to this A-list party, he'd RSVP'd no. That would make the evening much easier to navigate. She'd make Mr. Johns a happy client and, most important, demon-strate to Matt Richmond that he'd unquestionably made the best choice in hiring her as an event plan-ner. Everything on the professional front was com-ing together nicely.

On the personal front, she'd finally heard from Joshua. He'd called while she was in the shower that morning, although when she'd tried to call him back, she only got voice mail. He'd assured her everything was fine. He had it "under control." The Fixer had contacted her as well, saying that it appeared Joshua had some gambling debts, but that he was paying them off and wherever the seven-million-dollar sum came from, it didn't seem to be real. The whole thing sounded a bit suspicious to Teresa, especially since the man never called back. He'd said he'd be in touch, but had done no such thing. In her limited experience, people like that follow through on their promises. For now, she had to trust Joshua to handle his own affairs. She loved him, but she couldn't be his perpetual babysitter.

Teresa's assistant, Corinne, ducked into her office and placed a coffee cup on her desk. "Here's your two-o'clock latte and your mail." Corinne pushed aside a pile of notes and papers from The Opulence event. "Also, you will not believe what's on TV right now."

"Please tell me it doesn't have to do with the retreat." This event had become so complicated it was like trying to fight off a dragon with three heads. Just when she got one thing under control, something else went off the rails.

Corinne's blazing red corkscrew curls bobbed up and down when she shrugged. "Sorry, but it has to do exactly with that. Come and see. It's best if you know now."

Teresa planted both hands on her desk and pushed herself to standing. Her lower back was stiff from sitting for too long. She really needed to go to the gym and get a massage and take a minute to breathe. Sex might not hurt, either. She could certainly stand to blow off some steam.

She wandered out into the main Limitless Events office. Normally the large and open loft space was abuzz with activity, but right now, everyone was in the far corner, looking up at one of the flat-screen TVs mounted to the exposed brick wall. Teresa hurried over. Sure enough, her biggest nightmare was playing out before her eyes.

The crawl at the bottom of the screen read: *Peter Bell, lead singer of rock band London Town, arrested for felony battery after altercation with fan.*

Teresa closed her eyes and pinched her nose in an effort to ward off the headache that was about to ravage her head. London Town was not only her headliner for the Saturday evening gala during the Richmond retreat, but it had also been a real coup to get them in the first place. They did not like to perform at private events, especially ones hosted by the rich and famous. She didn't even need to know Mr. Bell's legal fate to know that there was no way his band could perform now. Even if the charges were dismissed or he was released on bail, the media backlash would be too much. Matt wanted no problems and this was officially a big one. Teresa had to find a top notch, A-list performer who just happened to be available on a Saturday night in a month. *Great.*

With no time to lose, Teresa hustled back to her

desk to go through her original planning notes and brainstorm. She might need to call Gideon Johns, since he had his finger on the pulse of all things music-related. But as she stepped inside her office, she realized she didn't need to think long. On top of the stack of mail Corinne had delivered was the latest issue of *Hundred Proof* magazine with gorgeous Jessie Humphrey on the cover. Jessie's voice was powerful, but like velvet, and she was one of the most in-demand performers around. Teresa had no idea if she was on tour or even in the country, but she had to at least look into it.

With a quick internet search, she found the number for Ms. Humphrey's management, who in turn referred Teresa to her booking agent's office. Teresa explained her predicament as succinctly as possible. "I realize it's incredibly short notice, but this is for a private retreat for Matt Richmond. No expense will be spared. Ms. Humphrey will have the most luxurious accommodations, we'll cover all of her travel and we'll have the finest production. Anything she needs, she'll have it."

"Send the offer in writing and we'll take it to her team. No promises. She is available that weekend, but that is highly unusual and she would typically be spending that time resting."

Teresa thought back to her conversation with Nadia and Isabel at The Opulence. "The resort has a high-end spa. We can book her any treatments she wants. And I can personally attest to just how relaxing an atmosphere it is."

"Like I said, send over the offer and we'll look at it."

Teresa sweetly said goodbye, then grumbled as soon as she hung up the phone. If she wasn't able to book Jessie on her own, she might ask Gideon Johns if he had any connections that might come in handy. But she'd wait to see if she could manage it. She hated asking anyone for a favor, especially a billionaire client like Mr. Johns. She needed him thinking she could move mountains if necessary. Speaking of which, she'd better knock out a few more hours of work before heading home to get dressed for Mr. Johns's party.

Seven

Liam had hoped to skip the Gideon Johns party, but Matt had talked him into it.

"Hey, stranger. What's up? We hardly spent any time together at The Opulence," Matt said when Liam climbed into his gleaming black Aston Martin Valkyrie. Matt had an extensive collection of cars and on a night like tonight, when it was just the two of them out on the town, they both agreed this was more fun than having a driver take them.

"I'm not the one who disappeared." Liam shot a pointed glance at his best friend.

"I didn't plan for things to happen the way they did." Matt kept his eyes trained on the road, but he shifted in his seat.

"Let me guess. You and Nadia." Liam caught Matt fighting back a smile. "You are playing with fire, my friend. I'm serious. There's no way this ends well for you."

The trace of happiness on his face vanished. "I know. I know. There's just something about her. She makes me happy. And the minute we're alone, we can't keep our hands off each other."

Liam had experienced that last part with plenty of women, but the part about someone making him happy? It had never happened. No woman had come close to making his life better. "Just remember that there's a person on the other side of this equation. If you hurt her, you're going to lose someone you obviously care about and the best assistant you've ever had."

"Got it. New subject, please. You and Teresa. Have you two at least reached a stalemate?"

"I suppose. She denies the affair with my father, but I'm not sure I believe her. I know I don't trust her."

Matt let out a deep exhale. "I'm a little worried about that, too, to be honest."

"You are? Why?" Matt was the guy who worried about too little. He was the one who had dismissed Liam's concerns about Teresa in the first place.

"Nadia overheard Teresa on the phone that day at The Opulence. She was outside, clearly trying to get some privacy. She said something about how she loved some guy and didn't want him to go to jail."

Liam knew he should have gone with his gut. Teresa was not to be trusted. She'd specifically told him that night at the bar that she was unattached. She'd even used the word *single*. And jail? What was she wrapped up in? "I had my investigator look into her. He's found nothing. And I told him to dig deep."

"That's weird. There's always dirt."

"Precisely why I'm sure that something is up."

"Maybe we need to take things into our own hands," Matt said, stopping at a red light. "And by we, I mean you."

"What? When?"

"Tonight. At this party. You're the one who has a past with her. I hardly know her and she's in my employ right now. You're the obvious person to try and get her to slip up and say something she doesn't want to."

Liam grumbled and looked out the window as Matt took the corner and pulled up to the valet stand outside the Chihuly Garden and Glass exhibit at the base of the Seattle Space Needle. "I was hoping to give her a wide berth this evening."

Matt put the car in Park and turned, clapping Liam on the back. "Sorry, buddy, but I need you to do this for me. If I'm going to have to cut her loose, I need to do it now."

"Fine. But you're buying the drinks tonight."

Matt laughed quietly. "Are you kidding me? It's a Gideon Johns party. It's open bar."

The two men climbed out of the car and began

their walk up the red carpet that led up to the museum entrance. The all-glass structure was a sight, a modern cathedral ablaze with light set against the backdrop of the night sky. Up ahead, Liam spotted Teresa, looking like a million bucks in a slinky but tasteful black dress. She appeared to be overseeing two women with clipboards who were likely the custodians of the guest list. She was abuzz with activity, smiling and chatting, giving directions and gracefully gathering guests to stand for photographs before entering the party. It might take some doing to get her alone tonight, but he had no choice. Matt was his best friend and he would not let him down.

Matt tugged on Liam's jacket and leaned closer. "Nadia's here. With her date." With a toss of his head, he indicated they were standing behind them.

"A date? Did you know this was going to happen?" Liam carefully craned his neck, spotting Nadia and her date several people back. The guy had his arm around Nadia and they were eagerly talking to each other.

"I knew. She told me in the office earlier. She said he's an old friend. In town for the night."

"Maybe this is a good thing," Liam said out of the corner of his mouth. "Maybe this will remind you that you need to move on. Nothing good comes of a relationship with Nadia that's anything beyond professional."

Just then Liam felt a hand on his shoulder.

"Look who we have here. Two of the most handsome men in all of Seattle." Matt's head of PR, Shayla, had inserted herself between Matt and him. It was so like her. She was beyond pushy.

"Hi, Shayla."

She unsubtly smoothed her hand over Liam's shoulder. "Hello, Liam. Looking dashing this evening."

"You as well," Liam said, not necessarily meaning it, but feeling that it was something he had to say.

"I see that Nadia brought a date. What a hottie he is." Shayla practically purred it into Matt's ear.

Matt shrugged his shoulder. "Shayla, do you mind? Liam and I were in the middle of a personal conversation."

She shook it off. "Oh. Yes. Of course. I'll catch up with you two later."

"The date thing really bugging you that much?" Liam asked.

"No," Matt said, with a tone that distinctly suggested he was nothing if not completely annoyed. "I just don't like it when Shayla sticks her nose in everything."

Teresa continued her work as guest-list spotter, identifying each guest before they reached her assistants, then slyly feeding them the name with a whisper. Teresa knew VIPs and they took great offense when someone didn't recognize them. No one wanted to give their name. Of course, that meant Teresa had spent hours memorizing names and faces, since she hadn't been back in Seattle long enough to truly know the current landscape of the wealthy and fabulous in the city.

Out of the corner of her eye, she spotted Liam and Matt. "Matt Richmond and Liam Christopher are next," she quickly muttered to one of her helpers, before turning her attention to the two men. "Welcome, gentlemen." She hugged Matt, then regarded Liam with a penetrating glance. He unsubtly eyed her from the top of her head all the way down to her perfectly pedicured toes. She felt naked. Exposed. In a dangerous, but delicious, way. "Mr. Christopher. I thought you weren't joining us this evening."

He shrugged. "What can I say? My best friend convinced me it might be fun."

"I assure you it will be exactly that. Please. Come in. The bars are right inside the doors, servers are bringing around small bites, and the band should be starting any minute now."

"Speaking of band," Matt said, "I heard there's a problem with London Town."

Teresa shook her head. "Already handled. I'm this close to booking Jessie Humphrey." That was a stretch, but she could afford to do nothing less than wow Matt Richmond right now.

"You got it fixed that quickly? Excellent. I'm impressed."

"All in a day's work." She dismissed it with a

ready smile, knowing it would take more like an entire week's worth of phone calls, begging and logistics.

Matt and Liam stepped into the party, but Liam turned back to her, taking her hand. It was only the tips of her fingers, but to Teresa's surprise, it sent a verifiable jolt through her. "I'm hoping you'll save a dance for me."

"You are? Is this part of waving your white flag?" The words spilled from her lips before she had a chance to really think about how rude they might sound.

"I try never to surrender, but I might be willing to give up some ground." He cocked one thick eyebrow for effect.

Teresa had to try very hard not to fixate on the curve of his lips or the appealing shadow of his facial scruff. Liam was so her type it was ridiculous. "Color me intrigued." She didn't offer more, and turned back to focus again on the guest list, but her heart was beating hundreds of miles an hour, like a jackrabbit with a bad coffee habit. What did Liam mean by that? Was he up to something? Or was he actually softening his approach? The latter, although a nice idea, seemed unlikely.

She helped with the next fifty or so guests, including Nadia Gonzalez and her unbelievably hot date, whom Teresa was sure she'd recently seen in a men's magazine. She couldn't help but wonder how Matt might be handling that particular development, although knowing the world of corporate PR, someone had probably arranged the pairing to give the illusion that Matt and Nadia were not a thing.

Teresa filtered through the party, stopping to make sure guests had everything they wanted and were having a good time. The band had started playing, but as was par for the course with most of these occasions, people were crowding the perimeters of the dance floor and not actually paying attention to the entertainment.

Teresa smiled and stood straighter when she saw Gideon Johns heading for her. Even in a crowd of fabulously beautiful people, Gideon stood out. He had a tall, broad frame, dark, warm eyes and a killer smile. He was the epitome of a truly dashing gentleman, the kind of man most women hoped would sweep them off their feet. He grasped her elbow and they exchanged kisses on both cheeks. "The party is amazing, Teresa. You've done a wonderful job."

Teresa saw a twinge of uncertainty on his handsome face. "But nobody is dancing and that has you worried people aren't having a good time." One of the first things Mariella Santiago-Marshall taught her in event planning was to acknowledge and address problems before the client had a chance to.

Gideon's straight shoulders relaxed. "Yes. What can we do about it?"

Teresa spotted Liam over by one of the bars, chatting with Matt. "I'll get it going. Don't you worry about that. Just, please, enjoy yourself." Before she had a chance to let her pride get in the way, she buzzed through the crowd and approached Liam. "I'm here to claim that dance you asked for."

Liam swirled the ice in his glass, looking down at her with his trademark steely expression. "We'd be the first ones out there. It's not really my style."

Of course, he had to put up a fight. Nothing about this could be easy. "I doubt that very seriously. I'm guessing you don't like to do anything that other people are doing. Come on." She plucked his glass out of his hand and set it on the bar. "Can you babysit his drink?" she asked Matt.

"Of course."

With Liam in tow, Teresa wound her way through the crowd. When she spotted Nadia and her boy toy standing near the dance floor, she saw an opportunity to help things get started a little quicker. "Come on. You two should dance."

Nadia looked at her date and he didn't hesitate to take her hand and follow along.

Teresa might have been in charge of their route, but when they reached their destination, Liam took control, coming to a stop and pulling on Teresa's hand and twirling her into his arms. He placed his hand on her back and drew her close with a definitive tug. His cologne filled her nose, and the feeling of his form pressed against hers made every nerve ending in her body come alive. She'd forgotten what it was like to be in a handsome, sexy man's arms. It had been far too long. He started their rhythmic sway and Teresa did her best to relinquish control and let him lead. It was very, very difficult for her to let someone else be in charge, even a man as commanding as Liam.

"You're a surprisingly good dancer," she said, raising her chin and speaking right into his ear.

"Why is it surprising?" He kept the side of his face close to hers. That stubble she'd been admiring scratched her cheek, and she enjoyed it a little too much. "Years of cotillion at my mother's insistence. She's very big on social skills and propriety."

"You just seem a bit buttoned-up, that's all. In my experience, men like you have a hard time letting go when it comes to anything that involves their body."

Liam cleared his throat and pressed even more firmly on her lower back. "Trust me. I have zero problem in that department."

A steady stream of warmth encircled her, like someone had drizzled hot honey all over her body. She felt her shoulders loosen. The skin of her chest and neck plumed with heat. "I'll have to take your word for it."

"You never know. Stranger things have happened."

Teresa wasn't sure what he meant by that and was honestly a bit scared to ask. If ever anyone needed proof that she was in over her head, that was it. She was scared of very little. "Why do I have the feeling you're trying to get something out of me?" she asked.

He spun her to the middle of the dance floor, and much to Teresa's delight, five or six other couples joined them. Off in the distance, she could see Gideon smiling. Her plan had worked. Which meant she could focus on Liam.

"Well, I do have a question for you," he said.

She really hoped this wasn't going to be more about his dad. She'd been clear with him that nothing had happened and the idea of rehashing it was tiresome. "Go for it."

"You specifically told me at The Opulence the other day that you're single, but I've heard that's not true. Why lie about it?"

"Heard from where?" Teresa attempted to make eye contact, but Liam's eyes were cast off to the side. She placed her fingers against his cheek and her thumb on the tip of his jaw, forcing him to look at her.

"People talk."

Likely story. "Well, I don't know who's gossiping about me, but I am as single as they come. I have no reason to lie about that."

"You sure? No special guy in your life? Someone you love?"

What exactly was he getting at? "Definitely not."

"I don't think I know you well enough to know if you're telling the truth." He no longer had any hesitation about confronting her with his gaze, his expression both dark and daring. It made her want to do dangerous, foolish things.

"We're in the middle of a dance floor in front of hundreds of people. Everyone is watching us and how close we're dancing." Their hips were already pressed against each other, but Teresa wanted to make her point. She angled her hip and rubbed up against the front of his pants. There was a distinct stiffening between his legs, which filled her with some feminine pride. "Do you think I would dance with you like this if I was taken?"

"That doesn't prove a thing." Liam made the mistake of pursing his lips and Teresa was stuck for a moment, staring at them, struck with a curiosity she had to quench. They were so perfect. Full. Firm-looking. And then there was the man behind them. What kind of kisser would Liam be? Reckless? Careful? Determined?

"Then this will." Teresa raised her hand again, this time to the side of his neck. She cupped her fingers around his nape and pulled him closer, allowing her eyes to flutter shut while she let pure instinct take over. She laid the softest, sexiest kiss on his lips she could muster. The sort of maddening kiss that kept a man coming back for more.

It was perfect. But she hadn't taken the time to calculate his response. His hand pressed against her lower back, making the move she'd made with her hips look like child's play. He tilted his head and urged her lips apart with his tongue, taking the kiss deep. So very deep. Teresa bowed into him. It was the only thing that made sense, especially when white-hot heat began zipping up her thighs and making everything between her legs ache for more.

She wanted him.

More than she'd wanted any man in a long time.

And that scared her. She wrenched her lips away from his and was jolted back into the present—where hundreds of people she should be entertaining and impressing were likely watching. What was she doing? Had she lost her mind?

"We can't do this…" she muttered.

"You kissed me, Teresa."

She stepped back, if only to gain some composure. "I know that. And now I'm not kissing you." She made only a cursory glance at his face, but she could see that it was colored with confusion. Of course he was confused. She was, too. She had to get to the ladies room and get her act together, ASAP. "I have to go." She turned and wasted no time hustling off the dance floor, leaving Liam behind to fend for himself. She greeted guests along the way, but only in the most superficial of ways, saying hello and breezing past. She felt like her heart was going to burst out of her chest.

Finally she reached the ladies room and ducked inside. Meanwhile, only one thought was running through her head. *I kissed Liam Christopher.* Unfortunately, the possible repercussions quickly followed. Liam and Matt Richmond were best friends. They'd come to this party together and Teresa had not only laid a serious kiss on Liam's lips, but she'd also just abandoned him on the dance floor. What was Liam's only logical action at that point? To walk back, alone, and join his friend, at which point he would most likely tell him exactly what had happened. She was quite certain that the question of her sanity would be raised.

How stupid could she possibly be?

She first peeked under the stalls to make sure she was alone, then wandered over to the sink and peered at her reflection in the mirror, muttering to herself. "You have got to get your act together. You have to." If anyone asked her why she'd kissed Liam, she would have to say that it was his fault. He'd practically dared her to do it. He was the one who didn't believe she was single. Speaking of which, who had told him that? And why was he interested at all in her personal life? She already knew that he didn't trust her, and she was well aware of his loyalty to Matt.

The bathroom door swung open and in walked Nadia. Teresa straightened, but something about seeing Matt's assistant made a tear roll down her cheek. Had she just thrown away all of her hard work over one moment of weakness for a man?

Nadia smiled at Teresa, but it quickly fell. "Oh, my gosh. Teresa. Are you okay?"

Teresa nodded and bit down on her lip, trying to force herself back onto stable mental ground. "I'm fine. It's just stress. A lot happened today. The party.

Finding a replacement band for the Saturday night gala during the retreat."

Nadia joined her at the vanity. "And then you topped it all off with kissing Liam."

"You saw that?" The more hopeful parts of Teresa's brain had thought there was a chance she and Liam had been tucked away in the darkest recesses of the dance floor. Apparently not.

Nadia nodded. "Afraid so. A lot of people did."

"Including Matt?"

"I'm not sure. I haven't talked to him. But I can tell you one thing. There are zero secrets between Liam and him."

Eight

Nadia would've been lying if she'd said she hadn't been shocked when she'd looked over to see Teresa and Liam kissing in the middle of a room packed with Seattle's wealthiest, most influential people. Neither seemed the type to let loose with such a public display, and what a display it had been—hands in hair, open mouths and, without question, there had been tongue.

"What do you think Matt will say?" Teresa asked, seeming a bit desperate.

"He probably won't say anything to you, but that doesn't mean he won't have an opinion about it. You might want to stay away from Liam as much as possible, at least for a little while. Now would not be the time to slip up."

Teresa snatched a tissue from the dispenser on the countertop and dabbed at her cheek. She'd stopped crying, thank goodness. "I think I'm being sabotaged. Liam thinks I lied about being single. He asked if I had a special guy in my life, and he hinted that someone is talking about me. I don't know who it could be or how that would even come up in the first place."

Nadia debated whether she should fess up to her misdeeds. Perhaps it was best to just let Teresa know that eyes were on her and she needed to be a lot more careful. "It was me."

Teresa blinked several times. "Excuse me?"

"I overheard your conversation in front of The Opulence. I heard you say, 'I love him. I don't want him to end up in jail.' I'm sorry, but I had to say something to Matt. This is his first time working with you and the anniversary retreat is immensely important to him."

Teresa folded her arms across her chest, pursed her lips and sucked in her cheeks. For a moment, Nadia wondered if Teresa was tempted to deck her. Nadia was not a cat-fight-in-the-ladies'-room sort of girl. "Can you keep a secret? Between us. I mean, you can't even tell your boss."

Nadia had to think about that for a minute. "You have to understand that my first loyalty is to Matt.

If you're about to tell me something that could hurt him, I can't promise to keep it to myself."

Teresa nodded slowly as if she was taking it all in. "Okay. I get that. Just know that the man I was talking about on that phone call was not a romantic interest. I was talking about my brother. He has a habit of getting in trouble and I'm afraid he's done it again. I'm really his only safety net." Teresa's normally strong voice began to shake. "My mother just isn't able to deal with stressful situations like this and so it all falls on me. I'm all he has."

Nadia and Teresa weren't close at all. In fact, they'd already had moments in their short working relationship that had been downright adversarial. But if Nadia understood anything, it was the pull of family, the deep need to do anything to keep them safe and okay at all costs. She stepped closer to Teresa and wrapped her arms around her. Teresa immediately lowered her head on to Nadia's shoulder. "It's okay. I promise. I won't say a word." She rubbed Teresa's back softly. "Is there anything I can do to help?"

Teresa stepped back and wiped a tear from her cheek. "Not right now. I have someone watching out for him and we'll see how it goes. The big thing I could use right now is knowing that I can lean on you when it comes to the retreat. I can't afford for anything to go wrong and I know you feel the same way. Can we help each other? Will you be my ally?"

Nadia nodded eagerly. "Yes. Absolutely. Anything you need, please don't hesitate to let me know. We both want the same thing. For Matt to be happy. Liam, too, I suppose."

"Yes. Their big announcement."

A woman walked into the ladies' room and Nadia smiled, but she knew she had to shut her mouth. Nobody could find out about the Sasha project. "Is that going to make it difficult for you to stay away from Liam?"

Teresa shook her head. "We're supposed to have one planning meeting about the presentation, but that's it. Otherwise, I'm going to stay as far away from him as I can. Apparently I lose all good judgment when I'm around him."

The woman who'd joined them in the bathroom emerged from a stall and came over to wash her hands. Nadia and Teresa took their chance to step into the adjoining lounge.

"So, who's the hottie you're with tonight?" Teresa asked.

Nadia chuckled. Women had been asking her that all night, any time Hideo went to the bar to get them a drink. "Old high-school friend. We were never a couple. Just good friends. From the chess club if you can believe that. We also did the mock UN together."

"So the beauty queen was also a brain?"

Nadia cringed at the label. "I don't know about being a brain, but school and hard work were always important to me. The pageantry was to make my mom happy."

Teresa nodded. "You and I have a lot in common. Most things I've done in my life have been to please my mom. Or to just help her get by. My dad died when my brother and I were young and I don't think she ever recovered from it."

Nadia had to admit she was getting a bit wistful thinking about her family. "My mother is an incredibly strong person, but the pageants were one of those things she had always wanted to do herself but never had the chance. I think she lived vicariously through me. It was fine, but it's just not how I want to be defined. Beauty fades. And I know I'm a lot more than some makeup and good hair."

Teresa dropped her chin. "Honey. You are way more than that. You are the total package. Brains and beauty."

Nadia smiled. "You, too. Friends of a feather flock together."

After the things Matt had just witnessed from his vantage point near the dance floor, he needed a drink. He wound his way back to the bar, holding his phone to his ear. He wasn't placing a call. He simply didn't want to be stopped by one of the many guests, any of whom could ask him a potentially uncomfortable question. *Is it true you're sleeping with your assistant? Or is she with the ridiculously handsome guy she brought to the party? Who is that woman Liam was kissing out on the dance floor?*

"A shot of Don Julio, please." Luckily, Gideon spared no expense at his parties, which meant Matt's favorite top-shelf tequila was available. He stuffed his phone back into his pocket and fished a hundred-dollar bill out of his wallet, tucking it into the tip jar.

"Wow. Thank you, sir," the bartender said.

"No. Believe me. Thank you." Don Julio was for sipping, but Matt knocked back the drink and shook his head. It was a jolt of warmth he needed, and smoothed his unusually ragged edges. Matt prided himself on rarely getting rattled, but watching Nadia slow-dance with her "old friend" had done something to him. The guy's hand had settled far too easily on the small of Nadia's back as he'd snuggled her close. They'd talked and laughed, every second of it an excruciating test of Matt's patience. He wasn't sure he'd ever had such a purely irrational and visceral reaction to anything. Even now, just thinking about it, made his pulse race and the blood course through his body like a raging river. All he'd wanted to do was march out onto that dance floor and claim what he wanted—Nadia.

But she was not his. She'd been very clear about that. Crystal clear. But even knowing that, he'd still had to force himself to turn away. He'd had to talk himself through not making a scene. Was he losing it?

He turned and ran right into Shayla.

"Great party," she said.

"Fantastic. Teresa does an incredible job."

"She did quite a job on your best friend a few minutes ago. What's up with that?"

Matt had really hoped he'd been one of the only people to notice, but, of course, Shayla had seen it—she had a knack for catching people at their weakest. Or most embarrassing. "I do not know. And frankly, it's none of my business." Although it really was his business. Teresa was working for him. He needed her focused on the job at hand. And as for Liam, well, Matt had never seen him so much as hold hands with a woman in public, so seeing him kiss Teresa had been a true shock to the system. Liam had offered no explanation, either, and had simply told Matt that he was calling his driver and heading home. Matt would've gone after him if Liam hadn't made it clear that he needed to be alone.

"Nadia seems to be having a great night with that male model," Shayla said, her voice dripping with innuendo.

Matt was not about to take the bait. "How could she not? The band is really good."

"Hideo Silva is even hotter in person than he is in pictures."

Shayla could be frustratingly transparent when she was trying to get in her digs. "That's not really my call." Of course, the mention of it had brought the vision right back into his head—Hideo lowering his head and speaking into Nadia's ear, holding her close. In his mind, Matt could see her laughing, tossing back her mane of thick blond hair, the one he loved running his fingers through. He recalled every lovely inch of the stretch of her neck. Kissing her buttery soft skin was one of the most sublime experiences he'd ever had. Matt was not the jealous type. He had no reason to be envious of anyone. He had the world at his feet. But in that moment, he had been certain that if the world hadn't been watching, he would have lumbered right over to Nadia, taken her hand and led her far away from the handsome guy she was dancing with.

Across the room, Matt spotted Nadia, making her way from the ladies' room back to Hideo, who was standing at the one of the high cocktail tables, staring at his phone.

"You'll have to excuse me," Matt said to Shayla, not offering any further explanation. He walked double-time, not bothering with the charade of his phone. He had to talk to her before she reached her date. "Nadia." He grasped her arm, but quickly let go, even though he didn't want to.

"Matt. Hi." Nadia's gaze flew to Hideo, then returned to Matt. She frantically scanned the room, obviously trying to take note of who saw them together. She kept her distance from him, which made part of him die on the inside. All he wanted to do was touch her. Kiss her. Hold her in his arms. He was in trouble. He knew he shouldn't be feeling this way.

"How's your night with Hideo? Shayla thinks he's hot."

"Shayla thinks everything with a penis is hot."

Matt laughed, which at least lightened his mood. "Very funny."

"It's true. I'm sure she has the hots for at least five or six guys at work. I'm positive she has the hots for you, although every woman at work has some sort of thing for you."

Was she trying to deflect to make him feel better? Was she trying to make a point that if he couldn't have her, there were plenty of other women he could have? "Shayla used to date my brother, Zach. If that's true, I don't notice it."

"Of course you don't." Nadia sighed and looked away for a minute. "I should probably get back to Hideo."

Once again, Matt was saddled with disappointment. "Don't go. Stay for a minute. Talk to me."

Nadia cast him a look that made him feel foolish. "Matt. What kind of person would I be if I just stranded him? He's here from out of town. He doesn't know anyone."

She was right. Matt needed to get a grip. But he also had to get these feelings off his chest. It felt like he was being crushed by them. He made sure no one was looking and took her hand, leading her to a corner. "I need to tell you one thing. I felt sick when you were dancing with him. I couldn't handle it. I can't handle it."

She narrowed her eyes on him and cocked her head to one side, her beautiful blond hair cascading down her shoulder. "Seriously?"

"Honestly? I was surprised how much it bothered me."

"You don't strike me as the jealous type."

"I'm not. But apparently all bets are off with you." He dared to step closer, hoping the darkness of this corner of the room afforded them at least a little privacy. "I saw his hand on your back and all I could think was that my hand is the only one that belongs there."

"Matt, we talked about this. I like you a lot, but we both know this won't work. I can't lose my job and you're not the kind of guy who gets serious, anyway. I'm a one-man woman and I don't do well with casual. It's just not in my DNA."

Matt swallowed hard, his mind racing. She had such a talent for pointing out every obstacle between them. "What if it was more than casual?"

"What? That's crazy? Like announce it to the company? You do not want to do that."

No. He wasn't ready for that. It would be reckless and premature. But he might be ready for something else—anything to prove to her that he really was serious about his feelings for her, even when he couldn't see a way to make it work between them. "I'm not talking about that. I'm talking about you and me taking a step forward behind the scenes. Away from the public eye."

"Like what?"

"Meet my parents. Come have dinner at their house."

Nadia didn't speak for several moments, just blinked like crazy. She turned away for an instant and when she turned back, she looked scared. "Shayla was right around the corner. What if she heard us?"

"I doubt she heard a thing. The music is loud. Just tell me if you don't want to do it and I'll never mention it again." Moments like this were the real reason he never put his heart on the line. He couldn't stand the thought of rejection.

"No. I mean, I'm not sure. Let me think about it, okay? I'll call you tomorrow?"

"Please. Think about it. I'm serious about the invitation."

"Okay." She stepped closer and kissed him on the cheek. "Try to have a good night, okay?"

"I will," he said, then watched her disappear into the crowd. Of course, that was a lie. Matt wouldn't have a moment of fun while Nadia was with another man in the same room.

Nine

The morning after Gideon Johns's party, Nadia woke to a text from Shayla.

Matt is going to freak out. I need Teresa St. Claire's phone number so I can get control of this mess. Call me.

"Good morning to you, too," Nadia mumbled to herself, sitting up in bed and leaning back against her upholstered headboard.

Following Shayla's unpleasant but completely in-character message, was a link to an online business journal article filed in the wee morning hours. The headline made Nadia's stomach lurch:

Liam Christopher to Unveil Sasha Project at
Richmond Industries Exclusive Retreat

She quickly scanned the article, which was mostly
direct quotes from Teresa. Apparently she had spoken to the reporter at the party and they had been
digging for details of the retreat. It was becoming a
source of gossip since so no one knew exactly what
was set to happen at it, only that an invitation was
highly coveted and impossible to get. The problem
was that Nadia knew very well that she'd been the
person to spill the secret of Sasha to Teresa. If this
was anyone's fault, it was hers.

Nadia had to get out in front of this and she
needed to start with Teresa. It was still early in
the day. There was a very good chance Matt didn't
know about this yet. Unlike a lot of CEOs, he made
a habit of keeping his phone in his home office
while he was asleep. The man suffered enough in-
terruptions in his life. He needed to get sleep.

She hopped out of bed, wrapped herself in her
robe and padded into her cute but modest kitchen
to make coffee. As soon as it began to drip into the
carafe, she dialed Teresa's number.

Teresa answered before there was a single ring.
"Nadia, I swear I didn't say a thing. You have to believe me. I would have called you earlier but I didn't
want to wake you."

"If you didn't say anything, then how do you explain what it says in the article?"

"I don't know what to tell you. You're going to have to believe me. I didn't say a thing. I *wouldn't* say a thing. We talked about this last night. I can't afford for a single thing to go wrong with the retreat."

"Did you do the interview?"

"I talked to that reporter for less than two minutes. He was lurking at the end of the party so I introduced myself, and when he realized who I was, he asked about the retreat. All I said was that it was going to be fabulous and people would be talking about it for years to come. I swear that was all I said. The word *Sasha* did not cross my lips. I have no idea where he got that other information."

Nadia sucked in a deep breath. The Richmond Industries main office was occasionally a leaky ship, and the information could have come from any number of people. For that matter, Nadia had no idea how tightly the information was controlled at Liam's company, Christopher Corporation. Still, there were a few indisputable facts staring her in the face. First, the article had only mentioned the name *Sasha*, and not the nature of the project. That much was good. The damage was contained. Second, Teresa had no real reason to sabotage the retreat or Sasha, so what she was saying had to be true. And third, regardless of those details, Nadia had slipped in front of Teresa and she had to come clean with Matt.

"Okay." Nadia pulled a coffee mug out of the cabinet. "I'll smooth things over with Matt, but I can't promise he'll be able to do the same with Liam. You might have to do that much yourself."

"I thought I was staying away from Liam. Remember? Giving Matt's best friend a wide berth so as not to look unprofessional?"

Nadia took a long sip of her coffee. "At this point, our first concern is keeping him from blowing his top, especially to Matt. I don't think smoothing feathers is an unreasonable idea."

"All right then. I'm on it. I'll need you to text me his address. It's Saturday. I'm going to have to track him down at home."

"I'll send it as soon as we get off the phone. Let me know how it goes, okay? I'd like to know where we stand."

"I will. And Nadia?"

"Yes?"

"I owe you one."

"Don't worry. I'm not a person who keeps score." Nadia hung up and glanced at the clock. It was only a little after seven thirty. She knew Matt's Saturday schedule well. He typically slept until seven, then did an hour-long workout, staying away from his phone and the news. It was his detox time. Which meant Nadia had about twenty minutes to get cleaned up, get to his house and convince him that Teresa had not sunk the ship. At least not on purpose.

She had no interest in talking to Shayla, nor

did she want Shayla to think she was ever going to adopt the habit of taking orders from her, so she sent her a text.

I have everything under control. Consider yourself out of it.

Teresa tried Liam by phone as soon as she got off her call with Nadia, but he didn't answer. She wasn't surprised after the way she'd acted last night, kissing him on the dance floor. Seeing her name on the caller ID was probably enough to make him turn his ringer to mute and block her number. He might even chuck his phone into Puget Sound. Which meant that she was going to have to track him down in person. She was going to have to swallow her pride, twice, up close and personal.

For that reason, she knew she needed to put her best self forward. That meant striking a balance between business polish and weekend casual— form-fitting jeans, her favorite Jimmy Choo black boots and a sleek black cardigan that showed off just enough of her assets to hopefully keep Liam off-kilter enough to accept her apology. Or more accurately, apologies, plural.

Coffee in hand, she raced over to Liam's through driving rain. She was still angry with herself for the way she'd acted at Gideon's party, although now that the fog had cleared and she had the perspective of a new day, she knew the reason she'd done it. She'd regretted *not* kissing Liam one other time in her life—the night they met. Regrets did nothing but hold you back as far as Teresa was concerned, and she did her best to avoid them by not being afraid to go for it. Trying and falling flat on your face was preferable to being left with questions. Teresa did not do well with the unknown or chances not taken. She always wanted to know what she was up against or what was out there in the world for the taking.

Liam's house was in Leschi, which was situated on Lake Washington. It was one of the most affluent areas of Seattle, like West Mercer, where his childhood home was. But Leschi was more diverse, more new money than old. Teresa had to wonder if this had been a conscious decision for Liam, in an attempt to distance himself from his father. Yes, Liam was a formidable businessman, but he was still working for his dad, still living in his shadow. Perhaps that was part of the reason he was so protective of the Sasha project.

Much like the man himself, Liam's house was an elegant fortress, with tall stone walls and a modern wrought-iron gate. She rolled down her window, heavy rain still falling, and jabbed the button for the intercom, then quickly pulled her arm back inside the car. The sleeve of her sweater was already soaked.

"Yes?" a woman's voice said through the speaker.

"Teresa St. Claire to see Liam," she called loudly, to avoid having to stick her entire head out the window. Several moments ticked by, the rainwater rolling into her car and dripping onto her pants leg. It would be just like Liam to send her away or make her sit there while she got waterlogged. But instead, the gate rumbled and swung open. Teresa rolled up her window and pulled up in front of the house. She turned and looked in the back seat for her umbrella, but it wasn't there. She hadn't been smart enough to bring a rain jacket, either, which meant she was about to arrive on Liam's doorstep decidedly less polished and put-together than she would have liked.

She sprinted to the heavy double doors, trying to dodge the rain. Luckily, the entrance was covered, but Teresa didn't have a second to compose herself. Liam was standing in the doorway, filling it up with his broad shoulders and formidable stature.

"What do you want?" Even through the deafening rain, Liam's voice boomed. As jarring as the noise was, Teresa couldn't help but be drawn to it.

"We need to talk and you didn't answer your phone." Still winded from her sprint from the car, she smoothed her wet hair back from her face.

"We have nothing to say to each other, especially after that stunt you pulled last night. Or should I say two stunts, after that interview you did? Are you trying to get Matt to fire you? Or is sabotaging me your primary goal?"

A droplet of water fell from the end of her nose. "Are you seriously going to send me away when I'm standing on your doorstep like a drowned rat? Can I at least have a towel and borrow an umbrella?"

His lips pressed into a thin line. The man wore his displeasure the way most guys wore clothes—out in the open for anyone to see. This was not the Liam she'd met that night at his parents' house. He'd changed over the last few years. He was harder, and not in a good way.

Finally, he stepped back. "Fine. But you're only staying for a few minutes."

Teresa ducked inside, but stopped on the area rug on the other side of the threshold. Liam disappeared into what appeared to be the living room, but she didn't follow. She didn't want to drip water all over the pristine dark hardwood floors in the foyer, or on the expensive leather club chairs visible from her vantage point. Beyond, a fire crackled in the fireplace and all she wanted to do in that moment was sit in front of it and have a polite conversation with Liam, but she now knew that wasn't going to happen.

He stalked back into the foyer with a fluffy white towel and handed it to her, then stood back, arms folded across his chest. Teresa gathered her hair in a bundle and squeezed it with the towel, unable to keep from admiring Liam, who was wearing a fine charcoal cashmere sweater and dark jeans. In terms of things she wanted to curl up with, Liam was now at the top of the list.

"I take it you read the interview," she said.

"You just torpedoed years of hard work."

She shook her head. "But I didn't. The word *Sasha* did not cross my lips. I swear."

"But you know about it. So why should I believe you?"

"Because believe it or not, Liam, I want you to be successful with your endeavor. I want Matt to be, as well. I need you both to walk out of the retreat weekend being nothing but impressed with me."

A grumble escaped his throat. "Kissing me on the dance floor isn't a great way to impress the man who hired you."

Now they were on to the *second* thing she was going to have to apologize for. How quickly this conversation was going from bad to worse. "So you talked to Matt about it?"

"I didn't have to. He saw it. Everyone saw it, Teresa. What were you thinking?"

Teresa looked up at Liam and those fierce eyes of his. Would she see a softer side of him ever again? Or was she doomed to get nothing but his steely exterior? The only way to find out was to put a chink in his armor, and her best weapon was the truth. "You want to know what I was thinking? I was thinking that you're one of the sexiest, most mysterious and interesting men I've ever met. And that the night I met you and you asked me out, the thing I regret most, aside from turning down your invitation, is not kissing you."

The instant she was done making her confession, Teresa realized she'd hardly taken a breath. Her heart was pounding as she waited for Liam to answer. React. Something. There was an edge of surprise on his face, but there was something else going on behind the shield of his eyes. He was thinking about what she'd just said. Thinking hard. And since no words were coming from his lips, she had no choice but to assume the worst.

"I don't know what's going through your head right now, but it's the truth, okay?" She took the towel and placed it gently on a console table next to the front door. "I came here today to explain myself. I swear I did not tell that reporter about Sasha. And I came to apologize. I'm sorry I kissed you, Liam Christopher. I'm sorry you're so appalled by the fact that it happened." She turned and reached for the doorknob, yanking the door open. The rain was falling even harder now, but Teresa didn't care, and rushed out onto the landing.

"Stop," Liam said. "Wait."

Teresa did as he asked, looking back over her shoulder at him. "What? Do you have something else horrible you need to say to me?"

He shook his head. "I wanted to say that I'm sorry."

"You're sorry?"

"For thinking the worst of you. I had no idea you felt that way about the night we met."

She turned and shook her head at him. "So now

that you know that I wanted you, you're willing to forgive me? I had no idea you had such a fragile ego."

"I don't. But at least I know now that you didn't kiss me for some ulterior motive. And I know now that I'm not crazy."

"Crazy about what?"

"For thinking we had a connection that night we met. All these years later and I was still doubting myself."

For some reason, Teresa had an awfully hard time buying the notion of Liam being anything less than supremely confident. It would take some time to get her head wrapped around it. Time away from here. Away from Liam. "Well, now you know what it's like for the rest of us."

Nadia made it to Matt's house five minutes later than she wanted to arrive. His security detail buzzed her through the gate and she pulled up in front of his palatial home. The last time she'd been here was the morning after the hospital fund-raiser, when everything between them had started to change. She'd once thought that going to bed with Matt would be like a dream, and although the actual event was even better than she'd ever dared to imagine, everything else had become more complicated.

She grabbed her umbrella, then climbed the stairs double-time, rang the bell and straightened her sweater. She'd gone with a cobalt blue cashmere V-neck and she could admit to herself that she'd chosen the garment for very specific reasons. Matt always complimented her when she was wearing blue and she knew he liked to admire her cleavage. He'd told her as much when they were at The Opulence. She needed to distract him while she figured out whether it was worth risking her professional future to wade into deeper waters with him personally. He was expecting an answer about what had once been unthinkable—dinner with his parents.

Carla, one of Matt's housekeepers, answered the door. His staff had once been kind to her, but there was now a distinct air of cold disdain. The only thing that had changed was that she and Matt had slept together and everyone knew it. Apparently they did not approve.

"Mr. Richmond is downstairs in the home gym."

"I'm going to go speak to him now if that's all right. This is a rather urgent matter."

"Mr. Richmond has instructed us to let you do whatever you need to, Ms. Gonzalez."

Somehow that was not reassuring in the least. "Great. Thank you. I know the way." Nadia left the umbrella by the door, then hustled down the wide central hall, past the great room, library and kitchen, to a back staircase that led to the bottom floor of the home. Matt's house was built into a hillside and he had turned this lower level into a bachelor's paradise, featuring a theater with a fully stocked concession stand and seating for at least twenty. It also had a rec room that rivaled the most extravagant man cave, with pool tables, arcade games, a full bar and a bank of flat-screen televisions for watching every game imaginable, all at the same time. At the very back of the house was an expanse of glass doors overlooking the pool and spa.

She admired the view for a moment before venturing farther in search of Matt. The tall trees and perfect landscaping were only barely visible on this rainy, foggy morning, but she still appreciated it. Her apartment had a decidedly less glamorous view of a busy parking lot, while this vista was peaceful and serene. It hinted at a life where there were no worries, but she knew that wasn't reality. Would this kind of life ever be for her? Not only did it seem impossible, but it also didn't even seem likely. She knew she didn't need any of it, and she also wasn't sure she wanted it. Rich people seemed to have problems that were infinitely more complicated than hers.

For now, she had to hunt down Matt. She was not looking forward to breaking this news, but she had to. Around the corner, she found him in his gym on an incline bench, doing chest presses with a barbell. He had his earbuds in, and she didn't enter the room, but simply stood in the doorway and admired him. His muscles strained against the sleeves of his black T-shirt as sweat rolled past his temples. His normally disheveled hair was pushed back from his face and that look of earnestness and concentration while he focused on his workout made her smile. For a man who had been given every imaginable advantage in life, he still worked hard. He always wanted to be his best. She could hardly believe he'd spent even a minute being jealous last night. Hideo was a sweet guy, a good friend and admittedly easy on the eyes, but he was no Matt, a man who was uncommonly brilliant and kind, handsome but not consumed by it. Matt had absolutely nothing to be jealous of.

Matt rested the barbell on the rack and sat up on the bench, dabbing at his forehead with a towel. He pulled out one of his earbuds and that was when he noticed Nadia. "Hey. Isn't this a pleasant surprise?" His heartbreaker of a smile crossed his lips. The way his eyes lit up made her breath catch in her chest and her knees come close to buckling.

"I wish this was a social call, and I hate interrupting your downtime on Saturday, but we have a situation." She walked into the room, every step closer making his pull on her a little more impossible to ignore. "I wanted to tell you about it personally."

He swung a leg over the bench, then got up and walked to her, taking a long drink from his water bottle. His shirt lifted, revealing an innocent sliver of his stomach, but it gave Nadia all sorts of ideas that were anything but pure. She wanted to thread her hands under that T-shirt and peel it right off his body. Then do the same with his shorts. Perhaps this should have been a phone call. "What's up?" he asked.

"Teresa talked to a business journal reporter at

the end of the party last night. He asked about the retreat and somehow ended up writing a story with the name *Sasha* in the headline."

Deep creases appeared in his forehead. "How did that happen?"

"She swears she didn't say a thing about it, and of course I have no way of verifying that, but she really has zero reason to talk about Sasha. But I do need you to know that the reason she knows about Sasha at all is because of me. I slipped in front of her when she and I had our meeting at The Opulence. We wouldn't have to even ask ourselves this question if I hadn't messed up."

"Are you covering for her?"

Nadia shook her head. "No. It's my fault."

"And what were the details revealed? I need to know how bad things are going to get with Liam."

"No details. Just the name. There isn't even any mention of it being a technology-based project. But I realize it's less than ideal. It's not what you and Liam wanted. And I'm really sorry. I messed up. I understand if you're upset."

A breathy laugh left his lips. "You're amazing. You won't let the blame fall on someone else, will you?"

"I own up to my mistakes."

"In a business where almost no one does that."

Nadia shrugged. "Don't put me on a pedestal for doing what's right. I really should have told you when we were at The Opulence." Heat flushed her cheeks as she thought about the things they'd done to each other that afternoon. And that night. And the next morning. That moment when he'd dropped to his knees in front of her and lifted up her skirt? She'd revisited it in her mind dozens of times since it had happened. It still made her dizzy. "I guess I was too distracted. By you."

"And do you still find me distracting?"

It would be so easy to lie and say no and walk away. But it went against everything in her nature to hurt Matt or to be dishonest. "Ridiculously distracting."

"And what about Hideo?"

Nadia shook her head. "He's an old friend. Nothing else. Don't let your jealousy show, Matt. You don't need it. You have everything."

"I don't have you."

Yes, you do. The words were sitting right on her lips, even when it was the most damning detail in her life. She could spend her entire day questioning what she was doing with Matt, but she knew at her core that her desire for him ran deep. "Things are complicated. We didn't think that part through."

He agreed with a subtle nod. "I know. But I'm ready to make things even more complicated. I was serious about you meeting my parents. I want it to happen. This week, if possible."

Nadia's heart cartwheeled and did a backflip. She couldn't help it. It meant a lot to her that Matt wanted to pull her into the personal side of his life, even when it could make things even messier between them. She craved messy right now. She craved Matt. "Okay. If you think it's a good idea, then yes."

"Good." A sly smile crossed his lips. "You know what's distracting? That sweater. You look unbelievable in it." He grinned and stepped closer until they were nearly toe-to-toe.

"I thought you might like it."

He slipped his fingers under the hem of her sweater and ran his fingers back and forth against the fabric, his knuckles grazing her bare stomach. "I'd love to kiss you right now, but I'm all sweaty."

Nadia put her hands behind her back, rose to her tiptoes and pecked him on the lips. "Maybe we need to get you into the shower and distract each other."

"You have the best ideas." He grabbed her hand and began walking to the back of the gym.

Nadia stumbled along. "Wait. In here? Really?"

"Yes, really. The best shower in the whole house is back here."

Sure enough, back behind the water cooler was a door into a bathroom that rivaled any fancy hotel Nadia had ever been in. With cool gray slate tile, a long vanity topped with Carrara marble and a glass shower enclosure built for two, she was in awe of how beautiful this room was. And that she and Matt had it all to themselves. So much better than a phone call.

Matt wasted no time while Nadia put her purse on the vanity. He kicked off his shoes and stripped off the rest of his clothes. He was already hard, making Nadia wonder what she'd ever done to be so lucky. He reached into the shower and cranked the water, then turned his focus to her, starting with her sweater, which he didn't toss on the floor but rather folded neatly and placed on the vanity. Nadia adored the attention, and the way the color in his eyes darkened when he looked at her as he removed each item of clothing. Her boots and socks. Jeans. Bra. And finally, her panties. She stood before him completely naked, feeling as admired as a woman could feel, and that was a feat on its own. He'd hardly touched her.

He opened the shower door and she stepped into the warm spray, her muscles immediately relaxing. Matt stood behind her, pressing his erection against her bottom. He placed his hands on her hips and began kissing her neck, using the gentlest touch, all while the steam began to swirl around them. "You are a goddess. You know that, right?"

She didn't really know that, but it was an awfully nice thing to hear. "You're so sweet to me." *You make me want to give you everything.*

He reached past her for a bar of soap and rolled it in his hands, his arms threaded under hers. He spread the creamy lather up her stomach, then over her breasts, his hands working in deft circles, stopping every few passes to pluck at her nipples with his fingers. Nadia reached above her head and wrapped her hands around his neck, giving him unimpeded access to her entire torso. She pressed her bottom harder against his length, rocking her hips back and forth. Matt groaned into her neck then rinsed off one of his hands. Moments later his fingers were spreading her folds, rubbing her apex in perfect circles. His other hand cupped her breast, pinching her nipple and making her skin impossibly taut. The heat in the shower was building and so was the pressure between her legs. Tighter. Coiling. Zipping from her nipple to her clit and back again. Over and over until the pressure won. She knocked her head back into Matt's shoulder and called out. He slowed the motions of his hand between her legs, but he didn't stop. He seemed to be reading her gasps. Her breaths. And reacting to every sound.

She turned in his arms and kissed him deeply, the waves of pleasure still lapping at her muscles. "That was incredible."

"I love the noises you make when you come. I want to make it happen again. And again." His hands were all over her hips and butt, his eyes still raking over her body.

"I want you inside me." Nadia smiled and handed him the soap. "But somebody needs to clean up."

"I'll be fast."

It was Nadia's turn to soap him up, spreading the silky bubbles over his glorious chest while his hands were working the shampoo through this thick hair. Even after that mind-blowing orgasm, she still hadn't had enough of him. She wanted it all. He rinsed off and turned off the water. They didn't bother with towels, just stepped onto the bath mat and immediately fell back into each other's arms. The slick, wet skin of her breasts met his dripping chest and they spun their way to the vanity, hands grabbing and pulling, water going all over the floor.

Nadia reached back for the countertop and Matt followed her lead, digging his hands into her bottom and lifting her. The cool marble was a delicious contrast against her skin. She wrapped her legs around his waist and dug her hands into his thick hair, kissing him, their tongues winding as water dripped everywhere. Her hands followed the muscled contours of his back. All she wanted was this closeness with him. "I have a condom in my bag," she said, reaching inside and pulling it out.

Matt kissed her shoulder while she tore open the packet. Then he stood back and watched as she rolled it onto his erection. He got even harder in her hand and that made her ridiculously impatient. Matt again grabbed her hips, this time pulling her to the edge then guiding himself inside her once she was in the perfect spot.

His first strokes were slow and deep, and Nadia wrapped her legs back around him. But she could tell that he was already close—his eyes were shut, and his mouth slack. She pushed back against him harder, encouraging him to go faster. He didn't need to be gentle. And he read her cues, driving into her, sending her back toward her peak.

Nadia planted her hands on the counter back behind her and had to smile when she saw the way Matt was mesmerized by the way her breasts bounced with every forceful thrust. He was going even faster now and Nadia was right at the brink when she grabbed his hand from her hip and placed his thumb against her apex. He needed no further instruction. Two passes and she was jerking forward, calling out again, Matt following, his breaths heavy and ragged as he pulled her body against his and they rode out the waves together.

Several moments of pure silence passed between them and all Nadia could feel was the warmth and security of his embrace and the way her heart beat so fiercely in her chest. It was like her own body was telling her everything she already knew on some level. *Hold on. You're falling for him. Hard.*

Ten

Nadia knew it was dangerous to allow herself to get excited by the prospect of dinner with Matt's family. Her heart and brain were at war right now, and she worried that this was yet another case of Matt being incredibly optimistic and Nadia ignoring the reality of their situation. She was not from his world. She was his assistant. It would be a monumental task to get his family to see her as anything more than a temporary, and quite possibly foolish, distraction.

Matt reached across the center console of his car and took her hand. "I don't want you to be nervous. It'll be fine. They're very nice people."

"Okay." Nadia didn't want to feel so on edge, but

she did. She'd changed clothes six or seven times before Matt came to get her, eventually deciding on a demure knee-length navy blue dress with a matching cardigan and pearls. Nadia didn't consider herself a flashy dresser, but this outfit was going for superconservative status and she didn't like it at all.

"You look beautiful tonight," Matt said. "I don't think I've ever seen you wear that before."

"The last time I wore it was to my uncle's funeral. I figured this was safe. I didn't want your family to judge me by my appearance. You know how I feel about that."

"I know," Matt said. "Just don't overthink this whole thing. It's dinner. Nothing more."

Nadia shook her head. "But it's big. This is a step forward."

"Think of it as the start of us being closer."

"Is that really what you want, Matt?"

"It is if that's what you want."

Her heart sank. She didn't want to be demanding or have to ask for things. She wanted this to be a mutual agreement, a conclusion they reached together. "That's not an answer."

"I feel like anything I say will be the wrong thing. The truth is that I get involved with a woman and I just see where it goes. I don't think about the destination." He squeezed her hand. "I just enjoy the ride."

Nadia let out an unflattering snort. "I bet."

"That's not what I meant and you know it. I'm

doing this because you told me that you needed more. This is me giving more."

She did appreciate that this was difficult for him. He wasn't the only one putting a lot on the line. "I know. And I appreciate your willingness to try." She only hoped it didn't blow up in their faces.

"That's all that matters." Matt took a turn into a neighborhood and the houses began to get decidedly larger, and were farther apart and much more stately.

"This is where you grew up?"

"Yep. My parents inherited the house from my mom's parents. My grandma and grandpa retired in Miami and left us to deal with the rain."

Nadia could only think about her childhood neighborhood, which would be best described as quaint. The yards were tidy and kids ran around everywhere, but it wasn't the land of fancy cars or swimming pools. It was a working-class area with grocery stores and strip malls and people doing their best to provide. She'd loved it because it had always felt very real. The world of Matt's parents was so polished, which she struggled with. He wasn't like that. He was genuine, honest and affable. Hopefully that meant he was a product of his upbringing rather than the mansion they were pulling up in front of, with its towering columns, countless sharp-peaked dormers with white wood shakes, hulking trees artfully lit up and a garage with five bays.

"Wow. It's beautiful," Nadia said, climbing out of

the Aston Martin. Matt was immediately at her side, holding her hand.

"Thanks. Now let's go meet my family." He led her up the stairs to a pair of tall glossy black doors. He turned the knob and they stepped inside a foyer so big it was like a ballroom. From the sky-high ceilings to the untold number of oil paintings on the walls, from the grand piano in front of the two-story windows to the endless stretch of shiny wood floors topped with Persian rugs, everything was pure luxury and elegance. "Hello? Mom? Dad?"

From around a corner, a man with a striking resemblance to Matt appeared, a cocktail in one hand. Nadia had seen pictures of Matt's father before. This was *not* Matt's dad. "Hello, Matthew. How are you?"

Matt dropped Nadia's hand and took a single step forward. "Zach. What are you doing here? I didn't know you were coming to town." Nadia had been right—this was Matt's brother.

Zach put his drink on a glass coffee table and held out his arms wide, but he struggled to stand up straight. He'd clearly been drinking. "Don't I get a hug? And an introduction?" He directed his gaze at Nadia and smiled, but there was something creepy about it. A chill ran down Nadia's spine.

"Yes. Of course. Sorry." Matt embraced his brother, but it was quick and there was nothing warm about it. Matt rarely talked about Zach, but Nadia knew some of the backstory. Zach had been a part of the original formation of Richmond Industries, but had left under suspicious circumstances after only a year. "This is Nadia."

Zach reached for Nadia's hand and kissed it. She couldn't get it back fast enough. "Oh, I know all about Nadia. I read *TBG*." He looked back and forth between Matt and Nadia and wagged his finger. "You two should really be more careful. You never know who's around with a camera."

Nadia pressed her lips together tightly. If this was how tonight was going to go, it did not bode well.

Zach tossed back his head and laughed. "I'm just giving you two a hard time. Come on. Let's have a drink." He waved them over to an adjoining room with a wide-arched entrance and a beautiful mahogany bar at one end, lined with tall upholstered bar stools. "I'm having a gin-and-tonic. I hope that's okay with you both."

Nadia took Matt's hand and followed him into the room, which was almost like a cigar lounge, with dark oversized furniture and a coffered ceiling. She climbed up onto the stool next to Matt, still trying to figure out what in the world was going on.

"I'm just so surprised to see you," Matt said as his brother mixed a drink. "How long are you here?"

"As long as it takes to keep you from destroying your company and making an embarrassment of the Richmond name by running around town with your assistant."

Nadia wasn't even sure she'd heard what Zach had

said correctly. Luckily, Matt had the courage to ask the question that had to be asked.

"Excuse me? What did you just say?"

Zach set the two drinks on the bar and leaned against the counter lining the wall. "You heard me. I can't believe you thought you could be the one CEO who could pull this off. The board is going to skewer you if you keep this up." He then set his sights on Nadia. "I heard you were bringing her to dinner with Mom and Dad and I had to step in. You know that they have a very hard time saying no to you, so I figured I would do it for them."

"Wait a minute. Where are they?"

"They're in Portland for the night. I convinced them it was best for me to do the dirty work and for them to stay as far away as possible." He turned back to Nadia. "I hope you don't mind having dinner with the Richmond family B team. My parents thought this was a safer move. Just, you know, considering all of the tabloid stuff. It really bothers our mother. And our dad, well, he's on Matt's board and he really doesn't want to have to answer questions about his son's womanizing ways."

Nadia felt queasy, and not just because she'd barely eaten anything all day. "Maybe I should go sit in the car."

Matt turned to her. "No. Stay. You need to understand a few things about Zach. If you look up 'black sheep' in the dictionary, you'll see his picture. He is not an accurate representation of the feelings of anyone in this family, including my parents."

Zach scoffed. "Am I the golden boy? No. That's only because I never had any interest in falling in line. That's only because I refused to be the number-two guy at Richmond Industries."

"You were caught doing drugs at work. You hardly ever showed up and when you did, you were drunk. You stole money from the company. From me. I had no choice but to fire your ass. You're lucky I didn't make a big spectacle of it," Matt said, his voice uncharacteristically bitter. "Why don't you tell Nadia what your current status in Mom and Dad's will is."

"This really isn't any of my business…" Nadia said, getting off her bar stool and leaving her drink untouched. "I'm not comfortable with this conversation. I need to go outside. At least for some air." What Nadia really wanted to do was shrink until she was nothing. Until she disappeared.

"Hold on a second, Nadia. At least let me walk you to the car so I can make sure you're okay." Matt turned to Zach. "And you. Don't go anywhere. We are not finished here."

Nadia led the way, walking several paces ahead of Matt. She knew she never should have let herself think this was a good idea. At every turn in her brief relationship with Matt, she'd known it wouldn't work, and yet she kept pushing. She needed to resign herself to the fact that they were doomed. This was not going to magically fix itself. There were too many forces against them.

She flung open the door and rushed down the stairs to Matt's car. The headlights flickered and the horn chirped when he pushed the button on his fob. Nadia climbed in on the passenger side and wrapped her arms around herself.

Matt crouched down next to her. "I am so sorry, but I promise you that my brother is a psycho. There's a reason why we have no relationship. My parents even wrote him out of a decent chunk of his inheritance last year."

"So then why did they listen to him? Why aren't they here tonight?"

Matt took Nadia's hand. "I think this happens a lot with families when there's substance abuse. Nobody wants to believe their child is a bad person. Nobody wants to believe their child can't change. My parents might get upset with him, but they love him a lot. And they continue to give him the benefit of the doubt, even when he's burned them many times." Matt turned his head and glanced up at the house, then looked back at Nadia. "You'll probably find this hard to believe, but he can be very charming. Just ask Shayla. Those two dated for nearly two years."

Nadia didn't normally roll her eyes, but she couldn't help herself. "Yeah, well, as near as I can tell, they deserve each other."

"I'm going to go back in and talk to him, but just

for a few minutes. He's too drunk for a real conversation, anyway. Will you be okay out here by yourself?"

She nodded. "Yes. But don't be long. I want to go home." She hated the way her voice wobbled, but she couldn't help it. She was upset.

"I know this was a lot, but I promise I'll make it up to you. And I'll fix things with my parents, too. You'll see—everything will be fine." He leaned into the car and kissed her cheek. "Be back in a few."

With that, Matt made his way back up to the house and Nadia closed the car door. She pressed her hand against the spot where Matt had kissed her, wondering why life had to be so unfair. How could two people possibly have so much standing in their way?

Matt stormed up the stairs of his parents' home. He could not believe how upside down this night had gone. His parents had been guilty of putting the blinders on many times when it came to Zach, but he couldn't understand how he'd convinced them that his desire for them to meet Nadia could be so awful. Yes, she was his assistant. But she was a wonderful woman.

Matt walked back inside and stopped short of slamming the door behind him. "I don't understand what you want from me, Zach. Just tell me."

Zach was now sitting on one of the sofas in the living room. He'd put his cocktail glass on the wood end table without a coaster. If Matt's mother had been there right now, she would have been having a fit. "I want you to take me back at the company. I want back in on the Sasha project. I was there when you first started talking to Liam about it. I want everything you promised me when we started the company. Notice I said *we*, not *you*. We started Richmond Industries together and you cut me out. You think I don't see how much money you're making? It's obscene. Flying around in your corporate jets and spending a fortune on parties for your famous friends."

And now Matt felt as though a light switch had been flipped. He could see everything. "You leaked the Sasha story. That was you, wasn't it?"

Zach knocked his head to one side. "It was hardly a leak. I only divulged the name. And it was just to get your attention. Unfortunately, you left me sitting by the phone waiting for a call. I'm surprised it took you this long to figure it out, but you never were the smart one."

"I'm not taking you back at the company. You know what you did and I'm not letting you back in. I don't care what kind of story you told Mom and Dad, but I'm not falling for anything you have to say to me. I'm just sorry you had to go and tamper with my relationship. What Nadia and I have is special and tonight was supposed to be a step forward and you've ruined everything. How can that possibly make you feel good?"

"It's all quid pro quo, brother. If you hadn't fired me, Shayla never would have dumped me. We were in love. We were going to get married."

Matt could hardly fathom the way he and his brother remembered things in such radically different ways. "Shayla never loved you. She saved her own skin so she could keep her career on the right track. She knew where the company was going and she wanted to be there for the ride. And it's paid off for her. Very well, I might add."

Zach got up from the couch and walked back over to pour himself another drink. "I heard you had her pull the *TBG* story about you and Nadia. Making her do all of your dirty work these days?"

"How do you know about that? Were you involved with that, too?" Just when Matt wrapped his head around one bizarre fact, another one came down the pike.

Zach shrugged and knocked back his drink. "Have you figured out who owns *TBG* now? Bo Wilson, my dear and loyal fraternity brother. Honestly, Bo has been more of a brother to me than you ever have."

Matt's headache just got a whole lot bigger. And he could no longer stand the sight of Zach. "I'm leaving now. I'm going to take Nadia home and I'm going to call Mom and Dad and try to unravel whatever web of lies you managed to spin tonight."

"You didn't give me an answer on the job. We don't have to actually work together, if that's your problem. Put me in Los Angeles or New York. We can stay out of each other's way."

Matt had to let out a breathy laugh, if only to alleviate some of the stress of the situation. "I can't think of anything scarier than you working for Richmond Industries without oversight from me. Neither one of those scenarios is going to happen. You're lucky I'm still willing to be cordial to you at Christmas. That's all you're ever getting from me." Matt marched to the front door. He'd had enough.

"I'll be sure to let Bo know that you liked that first story he ran about you and Nadia," Zach called just as Matt was opening the door.

"What does that mean?"

Zach shrugged, his trademark move. He always did everything he could to appear innocent and clueless when he was anything but. "I'm just saying you never know when Bo might run another story. Nadia is so pretty. She really should have her face all over the *TBG* website so people can admire it."

"Stay away from Nadia."

"I don't have to be near her to hurt her. Or hurt you, for that matter."

Matt took one more step back toward Zach. His heart was pounding in his chest. He clenched his fists tight. If he was the type of guy to throw a punch, he would have done it right then and there, if only to knock that smug look off Zach's face. "Do not threaten me."

"I guess we'll have to see what happens. You know where to find me if you change your mind."

At that, Matt turned and made his real departure, this time slamming the door, not that it likely mattered to Zach. His mind was racing, but he knew one thing. He could not tell Nadia about what his brother had said. It would only hurt her. It would only hurt *them*. Things were still so new and tenuous between them. He wanted the chance to keep going, even when the world was throwing roadblocks in their way.

Matt climbed into the car. Nadia was in the same position, arms wrapped tightly around herself. He started up the engine and sped out of the driveway. "I'm so sorry about tonight, and my brother. That did not go the way I planned it to. Obviously. You need to know that he really is a big liar. Nothing he said tonight was right."

"Is that really true, Matt? I mean, he's said things that you and I have both thought. I'm sure your parents wanted no part of having me over to the house. I'm sure they're hoping that I'll end up being a passing fancy. That you'll move on to a different assistant and I won't be in your life anymore. That doesn't speak well for us having a future, Matt. It's sweet that you're all caught up in this idea, but I don't think it's going to work."

Matt had to wonder whose side Nadia was on. He wasn't about to give up so easily. If nothing else, he had to do it on principle. He and Nadia had done nothing wrong. Their relationship was built on mutual respect, admiration and consent. Yes, she wanted a lot more than he normally gave, but he wasn't ready to quit. Not yet. "I'm serious about Zach. He is a weasel. And he can say whatever he wants, but it's not going to change what's between us. It doesn't matter."

"But it does matter. Family is hugely important to me, Matt. I'm not only not off to a great start with yours, but tonight also felt like the universe trying to send a message that we can't have a real future together."

Matt had never been so frustrated in all his life. He pulled up to a red light and turned to Nadia. "I care about you. A lot. I'm not ready to give up on you, as long as you aren't ready to give up on me. Have you lost all faith in me? Just because of one conversation with my horrible brother?"

Nadia smiled and looked down at her lap. "I'm not ready to give up on you."

"Even after tonight?"

She sucked in a deep breath and looked out the window. "I guess not even after tonight. But I do want you to talk to your parents. If they aren't on board, we need to have a serious conversation."

The light turned green and Matt whizzed through the intersection. "Absolutely. My sentiments exactly. Tomorrow I will clear the air with them, we'll get it all straightened out and we can just pretend that tonight did not happen." *I know that I'd certainly like to forget it.*

"If you say so."

Matt was coming up on the turnoff to drop Nadia back at her place, but he didn't want to say goodbye. Not like this. Not after the night they'd had. Plus, they hadn't eaten, and he was starving. "Want to grab some takeout and bring it back to my place?"

"I *am* hungry. You promised me dinner."

Matt grinned and reached over for Nadia's hand. "Awesome. Chinese or Thai?"

"Thai. Definitely."

"And I want you to stay over. The whole night. No sneaking out in the dark."

"What about when your staff arrives in the morning? They all give me the evil eye when I'm there. Nobody thinks we're right together."

"But I think we're right together. And I think you think that, too. That's all that matters. I don't care about anything else."

Eleven

Liam could not get Teresa off his mind—probably because there was so much to think about. If she hadn't come to visit him last weekend, he would mostly have their kiss to ponder. What a kiss it had been, like the entire world opening up, her beautiful body bowing into his, soft and luscious and wanting more. Just as quick, she'd pulled away, shocked and surprised, darting across the dance floor and disappearing into the dark recesses of the party.

But the next day she'd given him an entirely new revelation, a new lens for viewing that kiss. She'd said that she regretted not kissing him the night they first met. He'd truly wondered many times if his attraction to her had been one-sided and, of course, he'd banished all thoughts of it when he thought she'd had an affair with his father. But she'd vehemently denied it, she had a plausible explanation, and most salient was the fact that his investigator had failed to dig up any dirt on Teresa St. Claire. If she had ever done anything wrong, he couldn't find it. Was it possible that she was exactly what she seemed to be—a driven and determined, but equally gorgeous and sexy woman? Or was something else going on behind that beguiling facade?

This was not a good time to be asking himself these questions. It was past 7:00 p.m. on a Tuesday and he'd just obtained a security pass to gain access to the waterfront warehouse near Pike Place Market, where Teresa's office was. They were set to go over the precise order of events for the Sasha announcement at the retreat. Then Teresa and her team could arrange the technical side—lighting, music, visuals.

Liam took the stairs up to the second floor, emerging in the office for Limitless Events. It was an impressive loft space with twenty-foot ceilings, arched windows lining the exposed brick walls and original hardwood floors. A dozen desks or so were neatly arranged in clusters. Teresa had quite a setup here. Liam could only imagine how bustling it must be during the day. For now, it was dead quiet, aside from a young man sitting at a desk at the far side of the room, the blue light from a computer screen illuminating his face.

"Hello?" Liam asked, his voice practically echoing in the open space.

The man looked up from his keyboard. "Can I help you?"

"I'm here to meet Teresa. She said she'd be waiting for me."

"In her office." He pointed to a glass-walled room with white shades pulled and the door closed. A soft glow came from inside. Someone was definitely in there. "I'd knock first if I were you."

"Of course." Liam strode over and tapped the glass door with his knuckle.

Teresa arrived seconds later, but she didn't open the door all the way. "We have to reschedule."

"What? Why?"

"Something came up." Her voice did not have its usual confident tone. She was rattled.

"Is something wrong? Can I help?" Liam couldn't help it. When he saw a woman who was upset, he wanted to fix the problem. Make it go away. Perhaps it was a conditioned response. He'd been doing precisely that for his mother since he was a little boy.

Teresa shrank back from the door. "Just go, Liam. Why would you want to help me? You don't even like me."

He took his chance and pressed on the door. Teresa was walking over to the window. Her office was mostly dark, the only light coming from the golden glow of the city and a lamp on her desk. "That's not true. I like you. We just have a lot of history for two people who hardly know each other."

She sniffled. She'd been crying, which was such a stark contrast to her nut-hard exterior. "You don't want to hear my sob story."

"What kind of man would I be if I walked away from someone who is clearly upset?" He ventured closer to her and placed his hand lightly on the center of her back. Just like during their dance, she leaned into him. "Tell me what's going on."

"It's my brother. He got mixed up with some terrible people. Two weeks ago I got a call from someone claiming my brother owed them seven million dollars. Turned out not to be true. Or maybe it was true because I just got a call saying he's been kidnapped and they'd call back with demands soon. It sounded like the same voice, but I'm not sure."

"Is this your brother, Joshua?" The instant the words came out of his mouth, he realized he'd made a huge mistake.

Teresa quickly turned her head and narrowed her sights on him. "How do you know my brother's name? Nobody is supposed to know about him."

Liam cleared his throat. It was time to come clean. "That day at The Opulence. When I first ran into you. I decided to have an investigator in my employ do a bit of digging."

"You did what?"

"I know. I know. It sounds horrible, but you have to understand I believed one thing and you were staunchly denying it. I had to know whether or not I could afford to believe you."

"And you were able to find out about Joshua? That shouldn't happen."

"Only a little bit. Only that you have a brother by that name. There was a record of his graduation from high school, but after that, it's like he disappeared. To be honest, I wondered if something happened to him."

She drew in a deep breath, seeming no less troubled. "It's a long story, but Josh got into trouble in high school, then went to Vegas and got into even more trouble. Drugs. The wrong people. By that time, I was working with Mariella Santiago-Marshall at MSM Event Planning in Santa Barbara. Your dad helped me get that job. I shared my problem with Mariella and she told me about a man her husband worked with. A man called The Fixer."

This was not a shock. The Marshalls were an immensely powerful family of considerable wealth. "I've heard of him. Unfortunately, most people in my world need somebody on their side to make problems go away."

"I was desperate. I had to get Joshua out of jail, out of Vegas, and away from these people. They were very dangerous. He took care of everything. He was supposed to make him invisible."

"Honestly, he did a really good job. My guy took two weeks to find what he did and it wasn't easy."

"The Fixer does a fantastic job. The problem is I

want to call him and see what's going on with Joshua, but I don't have the money to pay him and I already owe him a favor that's to be determined. That's a scary proposition in its own right. There's no telling what he's going to ask of me." Teresa began pacing back and forth across the hardwood floors.

Meanwhile, Liam was hard at work thinking of a way out of this. "Let me call my guy. He's not familiar with the situation, but I'm sure you can get him up to speed quickly and you won't need to worry about paying him or owing anyone a favor."

"Not even to you?"

It would have been so easy to take advantage of this situation, but Liam's heart truly went out to Teresa. "Not even to me."

Teresa dropped her head to one side in doubt. "Now why would you do that for me? Two weeks ago, you hated my guts. You tried to get me fired."

Liam swallowed back his pride. He'd messed up. He knew that now. He should have cleared the air with her first before he'd gone to Matt. "So give me a chance to make it right. I'll call him. Let's make sure your brother is okay."

Teresa pressed her lips together, regarding him. She scanned his face like she was searching for something she desperately needed. What was this pull that she had on him? Why was his only desire to gather her up in his arms and see where a kiss could go?

"Okay. Do it."

Liam pulled out his phone and called his guy, who answered right away. "Liam. Nice to hear from you."

"Thanks. I have a friend who's in a real bind and we need your help. She received a phone call saying that her brother has been kidnapped, but she's not sure it's real. We need to find out what the situation is."

"Yeah. Of course. Can you put me on the phone with her so I can find out the details?"

Liam offered his phone. "He wants to talk to you. Get the info on your brother."

She seemed unsure at first then snatched the phone from his hand. "Hello?" She nodded and walked behind her desk. After a minute, she started to rattle off everything she'd said to Liam, along with Joshua's last known address, his cell number, a current photo and the name of a friend he spent time with. "Okay. Thanks." She stared at the phone for an instant, then turned her gaze to Liam. "He's going to call back." There was something so vulnerable in her eyes. She was genuinely petrified. It made him want to protect her from everything. "He said he has a contact where Joshua is. He said it could take anywhere from a few minutes to a day."

Liam nodded, understanding what a delicate situation she was in. Hell, *they* were in. He was involved now, too. He wanted this to work out okay. "It'll be okay. You just need to find a way to relax."

"I don't think I can do that. Not until I know he's okay." Teresa began pacing and Liam took the chance to remove his jacket and sit on the sleek black leather sofa in her office. The appeal of her form in motion was impossible to ignore—shapely legs that seemed to go on forever, hips that filled out her slim black skirt perfectly and just enough hint of the rest of her figure through a sheer white blouse to make him a little crazy. "What if it really takes a whole day? I won't be able to sleep at all. Not a wink. You don't have siblings, do you?"

Liam shook his head. "Nope. Only child. I always wanted a brother or sister though."

"Careful what you wish for. They can be wonderful, but they can make you crazy. I swear."

Just then, Liam's phone rang. They both jumped. Teresa ran out from behind her desk to Liam. Sure enough, the caller ID told Liam it was his guy. "Is there an update?" Liam answered.

Teresa held on to his arm, her eyes darting back and forth over his face. "What is he saying?"

Liam closed his eyes and tried to concentrate while his guy told him everything. "Okay. Thanks. I'll let her know." He stuffed his phone into his pocket. "He's okay. They tracked his phone's GPS and then got visual confirmation. He was with his friend at some bar. Not sure why he doesn't answer his phone, but I figured you can find that out later."

She dropped to a crouching position, dug her hands into her thick blond hair and began to sob.

Liam dropped to his knees. "What is it? Are you okay?"

No answer came. She was crying so hard that she was gasping for air.

Liam did the only thing he could think to do. He took her in his arms and rubbed her back. "Shh. Shh. It's okay." She sagged against him, crying and trembling. It was as if it was the most natural thing in the world. The only thing that made sense. She held on to him like he was the only thing worth having. He loved the feeling of being there for someone. He always had.

Being in Liam's arms on the floor of her office was the last place Teresa had expected to end her day. But here she was, desperate for air and swallowing back her tears. Liam had been a rock for her. Joshua was okay. She still didn't know what was going on with him, but he was safe. "I'm so sorry. I don't know what came over me. I'm just so relieved. I know we only had to wait a few minutes, but it felt like forever."

"I can only imagine. The important thing is he's safe."

She eased back her head and looked at him. Liam was a puzzle if ever there was one. Who knew there was such a deeply sweet and caring side of him? "Thank you for helping me. I don't know what I would have done if you hadn't been here. I really didn't want to have to call The Fixer. I don't know how I'll ever repay you."

"I don't care about evening the score, Teresa. You

can repay me by allowing me to call a real truce. I don't want our relationship to be contentious anymore."

A smile played at the corner of her lips. "Are you saying you want to be friends?" She sat a little straighter and smoothed her hand over the lapel of his jacket, wishing she could explore everything that was underneath it. "Friends don't kiss each other on the dance floor. Especially not the sort of kiss we had."

"Unless they're friends with benefits," he quipped.

They were both taken aback by his comment, eyes searching, neither speaking. Liam did not let down his guard like this, at least not that Teresa had ever seen. Was he caught up in the moment? Or was there something else going on here? Was this a dream?

"I've never had a friend like that. Tell me how that works."

Liam's eyelids became heavy. He reached over and threaded his fingers between hers then lifted her hand to his lips, leaving behind a tingle that managed to find its way to the most sensitive parts of her body. He didn't take his eyes off her. He merely left their connection to smolder. "I imagine it's like any other friendship. You make each other happy. You blow off steam together." He turned over her hand and kissed her wrist, closing his eyes and savoring the moment as if her skin was the most heavenly thing his mouth had ever touched.

Teresa sucked in a breath, mesmerized by his lips, his dark features, the boundless sexiness of Liam. She did not consider herself a seductress, but damn, she felt sexy, like an entirely different woman when she was around him. Between the intense relief she'd felt at knowing Joshua was okay and knowing that Liam wanted to be friends, that he didn't hate her, she had no reason to leave up her defenses any longer. She could finally follow through on everything she'd started with that kiss.

"I want you, Liam."

"I want you, too." He cupped the side of her face and drew her closer, kissing her. Their tongues found each other, tentatively at first. Gently. Softly.

It was quite possibly even sexier than their first kiss, but it wasn't enough. She wanted more. She wanted to flatten him against the floor and tear off his clothes. She wanted the same from him. She shifted to her knees. He followed, not allowing their kiss to end. They held on to each other, standing for only an instant before collapsing on the couch. Teresa scrambled to straddle his lap, hiking her skirt up to her hips. Liam sat forward and hurried his shoulders out of his charcoal suit coat, tossing it aside. Finally she could get him out of that crisp white shirt, her hands going faster than they ever had before. She tore back the garment, lowered her head and kissed his chest, letting her hands roam his warm skin and firm muscles, twitching with electricity. Liam had both hands on her bottom, bunching her skirt up at her waist and sliding his fingers into the back of her panties. They curled into her flesh, pulling her closer. She spread her knees farther, sinking forward until she could feel his hard erection against her apex.

They began to rock against each other. Just this limited amount of touching left Teresa feeling like she might come. She could only imagine what it was going to be like when she finally had him out of those pants. Breaking their kiss, she sat back and began to unbutton her blouse. Liam's hands shifted to her hips and he slid a little lower on the cushion, letting her put even more of her body weight against his length. The tension between them was such a delicious form of torture, Teresa was caught up in the push and pull of wanting him inside her so badly she couldn't think straight, and wanting to draw this out for as long as it could possibly last.

As soon as her blouse was residing on the floor, she reached back and unhooked her bra, then let it fall forward, ruffling it from her arms.

Liam shook his head, his eyes admiring. He was pleased. "You are so beautiful. Truly beautiful." He took her breasts in his hands and rolled her nipples between his fingers.

"And you're making me crazy, Liam. I want you. Now." However much it pained her to do it, she climbed off his lap and quickly rid herself of her skirt and panties. She grabbed her purse and pulled a condom out of an inside pocket. Meanwhile,

Liam had unbuckled his belt, unzipped his pants and raised his hips to wriggle his remaining clothes to the floor.

He sat, waiting with knees apart, his impressive erection on full display. Even from a few feet away, she could see how hard he was for her and she couldn't wait to have every inch of him. She stepped closer and took him in her hand, stroking firmly from base to tip. Every part of him she touched was hard and hot. She wanted that fire. She needed it. He closed his eyes and knocked his head to one side, drawing a slow breath through his nose.

"Never stop touching me like that," he muttered, his voice coming from the deepest parts of his throat.

"Something tells me you'll like this even better." Teresa had other plans. She tore open the packet, rolled on the condom and straddled his lap, guiding him inside. She sank down onto his body, her mind a riot of thoughts about how good he felt and how unlikely this scenario was. She never thought she and Liam would be having sex in her office. Fantasized, yes, but reality? She would have put money on it never happening.

They began to move together, falling into sync, a perfect rhythm. Teresa knew this wouldn't take long. Liam kissed her neck then angled his head lower, swirling his tongue around her nipple. She curled her fingers into his firm shoulders, rolling her hips against him, over and over again.

"You feel amazing," he said, his breaths already shallow. "But I need you to know something."

"What?"

"As soon as I make you come, we're putting our clothes back on and we're going to my place. I want you in my bed." It wasn't an invitation or a suggestion. Liam was issuing an order. Teresa, despite never wanting to take directives from any man, couldn't have been more turned on.

"We were supposed to get some work done tonight." She kissed him, knowing that work was the absolute last thing she cared about.

Liam laughed quietly against her lips. "You think I care about that? Because I don't. Not when I know I can have you at my mercy all night long."

Twelve

Two days after his run-in with Zach, his brother made good on his not-so-subtle threat to sabotage Matt and Nadia's chances at happiness by planting a story on *TBG*. The headline was so much worse than Matt could have ever imagined: "Beauty and the Boss Part Two: Playing Every Angle."

This time, the story was all about smearing Nadia and her name. Everything was twisted to show her in the most negative light imaginable. It talked about her beauty-pageant days, and how no one would have ever thought a woman like that would end up with so much responsibility and such a high-pressure job. It suggested that she was play-ing Matt and Hideo against each other and included photos from the night of Gideon's party, showing her in what could be construed as romantic situations with each of them. It mentioned the car Matt had given to Nadia as a bonus, suggesting, exactly as they'd feared, that it was given to her in exchange for sexual favors. It said that Matt was considering Nadia for a huge promotion and bonus, both of which were absolute lies, but he knew now that Zach would do anything to get back at him.

To make matters even worse, the story had gone live at 8:59 a.m., Seattle time, precisely when everyone at Richmond Industries would be sitting down at their desk, most of them checking email and online news before digging into the meat of their day. Matt could already hear the commotion out in the hall. His employees were milling about and talking, unsubtly walking past his corner of the office and glancing over before offering a phony wave and making a quick escape. Nadia had gone to the ladies' room and would likely be back any minute now.

Matt had to act, and quickly. He picked up his office phone and buzzed Shayla's extension. "Let me guess. The *TBG* story. I just finished reading it."

"What the hell, Shayla? How can they run this stuff? Am I going to have to call my lawyer?"

"It's not a bad idea, but you know that they can get away with saying a lot of stuff. And I mean, how much of the story is inaccurate? From where I'm sitting, most of it is pretty well on the mark."

"I am not considering Nadia for a big promotion or raise. That part is completely fabricated."

"Can you prove that you've never talked about it?"

"How do I go about proving that?" Plus, Matt knew the reality. He had discussed a raise with Nadia and she'd said no, wanting to avoid a situation exactly like the one they were in.

"You don't. Which is exactly why they published it."

Matt grumbled, beyond frustrated. "Can you make it go away?"

"I can try. But perhaps you should consider the fact that Nadia has become a liability. That's one way to make the problem go away for good. She's already worked for you longer than any other assistant. Nobody will bat an eye if you hire someone new. *TBG* will move on to the next story."

Matt glanced at his laptop and that's when he saw new email messages start to pop up, all from Richmond Industries board members, all with subject lines pertaining to the *TBG* story. "I'm going to pretend you didn't say that. Just please do your best, okay?"

"I always do. Is there anything else?" Shayla asked.

"No. Thank you." Matt hung up the phone and dared to open one of the emails. It very plainly stated that there was great concern about Matt's assistant and perhaps Matt needed to quietly have HR arrange a severance package so Ms. Gonzalez could move on with her life and stop causing the company undue bad publicity.

Matt didn't even have a chance to look at the rest of the messages before Nadia was in his office. "Did you see?" Just like that day at The Opulence, she had her phone in hand, and thrust it into his line of sight, confronting him with the ugliness of tabloid news. "My sister has already seen it. She said people in her dorm asked her about it. It's only a matter of time before my parents see this. They made me look like a gold digger, Matt. They made me look like a ditzy blonde. I don't know what to do." She sank down into the chair opposite his desk and stared at her phone again, flicking at the screen and shaking her head.

Matt pushed back his chair and rushed over to Nadia, taking her phone from her and placing it facedown on his planner. "Don't look at that anymore. Nothing good comes of it." He perched himself on the edge of his desk.

"This is just going to keep happening. It's not going to stop. It doesn't matter that I work hard or that I'm smart. They can paint me any way they want. They can make me look like an idiot beauty queen with designs on a very wealthy and powerful man and there's nothing I can do to stop it."

"I've already talked to Shayla. I'll call my lawyer if that will make you feel better. Nothing stops something like this better than a lawsuit. These tabloids are cowards, deep down."

"Shayla can't put out every fire there is, Matt. I already promised her she wouldn't have to do this again and now it's happening all over again."

"What do you mean you promised her it wouldn't happen again?"

Nadia sighed deeply and looked up into his eyes. "After The Opulence. That first morning after your emergency trip to Miami? When I told you that one of my coworkers had given me a hard time? That was Shayla."

Matt felt his jaw go so tight it was as if it was wired to his skull. "I'll talk to her. I'll get it straightened out."

"No. Matt." Nadia scooted forward on her chair and placed her hand on his arm. "I don't want you to talk to Shayla. She might not be my favorite person, but she has a hard job and we both know it isn't fair she has to deal with this. She should be concentrating on the good things the company does, like the Sasha project or the retreat. She shouldn't have to spend her days fighting off pulpy stories like this."

"She's my employee. She'll do whatever I ask her to do."

Nadia shook her head. "That's not very fair. She's worked for you for five years. I think she's earned better treatment than this."

"I don't understand what you're saying, Nadia."

"I hate to say it, but this time it might be best for us to stay away from each other, at least for a little bit. Maybe permanently. And I feel like the writing is on the wall. I can't work for you anymore. As much as I hate to say that."

"What do you want to do? I can transfer you into another division."

"You know how that's going to look. Like you're just finding a way to keep your girlfriend around."

Girlfriend. "I've never heard you refer to yourself like that."

A look of panic crossed her face. "Oh, God. I'm sorry. That was presumptive. I know that what we had was just casual. You were very clear about that."

"No. No. I like it. I like the idea of you being my girlfriend."

Just then there was a knock on Matt's door. It was Shayla. Matt waved her in. "Can you and I talk in private for a moment?" she asked.

"Whatever you have to say to me, you can say in front of Nadia."

But Nadia was already getting up from her chair. "No. No. It's okay. I need to get back to my desk, anyway. We'll finish this conversation later." She scrambled out of the room, closing the door behind her.

He turned his attention to Shayla. "Do you have an update on *TBG*? Are they taking down the story?"

"Actually, no. They are refusing to take my call. And I don't know if you've taken a gander at your email, but the board is pretty up in arms over this whole thing and they're all coming to me, demanding an explanation."

"Well? What are you telling them?"

"That it's not my fault a tabloid decided to run a story about one of the wealthiest men in the country having an affair with his beauty-queen assistant. Matt, you pay me the big bucks to keep your company in the best possible light. That means telling you things you don't want to hear. She has to go. It's the only way forward. It's the only way you salvage the company and its future."

Matt didn't even want to think about it. It made him sick to his stomach. "A leave of absence. Paid."

Shayla folded her arms across her chest. "Obviously this is not my call nor my area of expertise, but this isn't really a professional infraction on her part. It's more a case of being a liability. You can't give a liability a leave of absence. You have to get rid of it. Or her, I should say."

Matt felt as if his heart was about to turn in on itself. He couldn't believe those words were coming out of her mouth. He couldn't believe the choices he was being confronted with today. "I'm going to need to talk to HR about a severance package."

"Do what you have to do, but I'd do it quickly if I were you."

Matt looked through his glass wall at Nadia, who was typing away at her computer and talking on the phone at the same time. He wanted to give her more, but he wasn't there yet. She'd been right all along. They'd had their fun. If only he'd listened to her weeks ago when she'd said they had to go back to nothing more than a professional relationship. This was his fault. And he had to fix it. Somehow.

Nadia did her best to keep her nose down and do nothing but work, but every minute of that morning had been painful. She couldn't stand any more accusatory glances from her coworkers. And Shayla? The haughtiness she'd displayed when she'd left Matt's office was unreal. Not that Nadia blamed her. If the roles were reversed, Nadia would've been mad and annoyed, too. This situation had been entirely avoidable—she and Matt knew what they were doing, and they had thrown all caution to the wind and done it anyway. She'd also had to sit there and not say a word when the senior members of the HR team had waltzed into Matt's office and hunkered down with him. They'd even drawn the shades, as if Nadia didn't feel like enough of an outcast.

Nadia's phone rang and she wasn't sure she wanted to answer it, but she saw Teresa's name on the caller ID and realized she really needed someone to talk to. Someone who wasn't afraid to be brutally honest, but who also had at least some of Nadia's best interests at heart.

"Hey," Nadia said, answering. She got up from her desk and wandered down the hall and ducked into one of the small meeting rooms, closing the door behind her.

"I saw the *TBG* story. I'm so sorry. They're such bastards."

"I know. I hate it. It's awful. My younger sister saw it and I'm just bracing for the moment my mom or dad come across it."

Teresa sighed. "I don't want to sound like a broken record, but I really am sorry. Is there anything I can do?"

Nadia didn't know where to start. "I have to quit my job, don't I? There's no way out of this. My reputation at this company is ruined. I will always be the woman who slept with the boss."

"Oh, honey. I wish that wasn't the case, but I don't really see another way through this."

The empathy in Teresa's voice really struck a chord with Nadia, one that brought about more than a few tears. "I worked my butt off. I was on my way. And now I have to start all over again just because I had a crush on my boss and I acted on it."

"You had a crush on Matt?"

"Yes. For all fourteen months I've been here. It's pathetic. I'm just drawn to him, I don't know what else to say. Not that it matters. It's all over now."

"Well, it doesn't have to be the end for you and Matt, does it?"

"Without a job, I'm probably going to have to move back to Los Angeles. Nobody is going to hire me. Not in Seattle at least."

"I'll hire you. Right now. Today."

Nadia managed a smile and swiped a tear from

her cheek. "You're sweet. And I know very little about event planning. I'm not artistic. I don't have a vision like someone like you."

"I can teach you."

"I don't want you to feel sorry for me, Teresa. Don't offer me a job because you feel bad."

"Look. I'm not. Just think about it, okay? It's not my place to talk you into it. Only you can decide what's best for you. And that goes both personally and professionally. You're an amazing, strong woman who got mixed up in a crazy situation. It could happen to anyone. The important thing is to come out on the other side of it even stronger and more amazing."

"Wow. Thank you for the pep talk. I appreciate it." She sighed for what felt like the millionth time. "I'd probably better go talk to Matt now. He's most likely done with HR and I just need to do this and get it over with."

"Good luck, hon. Call me if you need anything."

"I will." Nadia hung up and walked back to her office. Indeed, Matt's door was open again and no one sitting in the chairs opposite his desk. She couldn't solve the questions of their relationship today, but she could undo at least some of the damage done to Richmond Industries. She could leave with her head held reasonably high. "Knock, knock." She peered inside his office.

Matt had his chair faced toward the window and was looking outside. When he turned to her and she saw the look on his face, she knew that he was aware of what she was about to do. "Hey."

"Can we talk?"

He nodded. "Of course."

She stood before his desk, much like she had her first morning at work, the first time Matt ran through the things he wanted her to do that day. She could remember the way he made her both nervous and excited. She could remember the way he made her laugh like a teenager, and how the longing for him, something that came from the very center of her chest, sprang to life. "I'm going to go write my letter of resignation. There is no recovering from what happened today. I need to start fresh at another company."

"I'm sorry to hear that, but I understand." It wasn't exactly what Nadia had hoped to hear, but she honestly didn't know what she wanted right now other than to leave the building without crying again. "Do you know what you're going to do for work?"

She shook her head. "I don't. Chances are that I will end up moving back to Los Angeles to regroup and spend some time with my family. I'll figure things out from there."

Matt's face fell. "We have a generous severance package for you. I need you to know that I fought for you in that meeting with HR. You got screwed in this situation and I feel horrible."

"I don't want the severance, Matt. It's only a mat-

ter of time before that ends up in the papers, too. It's
best if it's just a clean break. It's best for everyone."

"But what about us?"

Nadia closed her eyes. Matt's pull on her was as
strong as ever, but right now it felt like it might flatten her. "I'm not made for this world. And you and
I knew this wouldn't last. There's too much pressure. Too many eyes scrutinizing us and waiting
for us to mess up. I don't want to live like that and
I won't. The reality is that this world doesn't oper-
ate the way it should. Hard work doesn't account
for enough." Nadia felt like she might crumple into
a ball. Every word was true and agonizing. "Between what happened today and your brother the
other night and me needing to be there for my family, it seems pretty obvious what the answer to that
question is, doesn't it?"

He shook his head vehemently. "No. It doesn't
seem obvious to me."

"Matt. Please. Don't make this harder for either
of us. You and I both know that I will leave here and
we'll be sad, but you'll move on. You'll be happy
and do amazing things and I'll enjoy watching from
a distance." The vision materialized in her head.
This was the end of the road for them. And it might
kill her. "You're not ready to get serious and I'm
probably too serious. I've spent the last fourteen
months pining for you and wanting you and wishing you would want me, too. And I got a glimpse of

that. We had a few weeks that were amazing. That might be all I get, but I don't regret it."

Slow as could be, Matt rose from his chair and came around to the other side of the desk. "All that time you've been here, you were pining for me?"

Nadia playfully slapped his arm. She was desperate for any way to lighten the mood. "Of course I was. And that should tell you that you, Matt Richmond, will be just fine. You will find an amazing woman and get married and have kids someday."

"No."

"Yes." She grabbed both sides of his face and forced him to nod in agreement. "I know you think you aren't that guy, but you are." She poked a finger in the center of his chest, right in the vicinity of his heart. "You are that guy in here. You just need to let him out."

"Nadia. Don't. Don't leave."

That was when the tears started and all she could think was that she had to get out as fast as she possibly could. "It's okay. I promise it will be okay. I'll come back to get my things some other time when you aren't here. Just so it doesn't have to be weird." She popped up onto her toes and kissed him on the cheek, then turned and rushed out the door, grabbing her purse and making a beeline for the fire stairs. It would be easier to cry her eyes out there rather than in the elevator.

And that was exactly what she did.

Thirteen

Liam was having a crazy busy day, but he couldn't stop looking at his phone, wishing it would ring. He was expecting a call from Teresa and, well, he'd be lying if he said he hadn't been looking forward to hearing from her. Even more so, all he could think about was when he would next get to *see* her. They'd had a whirlwind forty-eight hours after the night they made love in her office, much of it spent in bed together. But then she'd had to go out to The Opulence to work on the retreat, and Liam was left wanting more.

There was a frantic knock at his door. His assistant, Duncan, poked his head inside his office before he could even call him in. "I'm so sorry to interrupt, but it's your father. He collapsed after a meeting in Portland."

Liam hardly had time to absorb the news before he felt as though he'd been punched in the stomach. "Is he still there?"

"He's almost home. I just got off the phone with his assistant. They flew him back on the corporate jet and they're en route from the airport. He asked that you meet him at his house."

"I don't understand. When did this happen? They're already sending him home? I thought you said he collapsed."

Duncan shrugged. "I'm so sorry. That's all I know right now. I called your driver and he's downstairs waiting for you. I've rescheduled your afternoon meetings. Let me know if you need me to move anything for tomorrow."

Liam collected his phone and stuffed it into his pocket, thankful to have an assistant who was so proactive. "You are amazing. Thank you so much."

"No problem, Mr. Christopher. I just hope your dad is okay."

Liam rushed through the office, trying to ignore the way people popped up from their cubicles with looks of horror or mumbled their condolences as he walked by. It was as if his father had died. Liam couldn't bear to think of that. He had to get to him as quickly as possible.

He hopped into the back of the limo and his driver pulled away from the curb. Liam looked out at the gray day. Parts of the sky were black as coal. He really hoped that wasn't a sign of things to come. His phone rang and he quickly looked to see who it was. *Teresa.* Her name brought a smile to his face, which sadly faded. He had been so looking forward to this moment and now a pall had fallen over it.

"Hello, beautiful," he said, leaning back in the seat and drawing in a deep breath.

"You sound stressed. Is everything okay?"

Old Liam's gut reaction to this would have been to not say a thing, but the truth was that he wanted to tell Teresa. He wanted to tell her everything. "My dad collapsed. I'm on my way to his house."

"Oh, my gosh. Liam. Is it serious?"

"I don't know. I guess it can't be too serious. They're sending him home."

"Call me as soon as you know something. I like hearing your voice. It's the best part of my day."

Liam smiled again, still surprising given the current circumstances. "I like talking to you, too. You're a good listener."

"When you talk. You are a man of few words." Teresa let out a breathy exhale on the line. "I'm glad you're going to see your dad. Please send him my best."

Liam winced at that, and he hated himself for having that reaction. He was convinced that nothing had happened between Teresa and his dad. But there was still this voice in the back of his mind whispering to him that women had lied to him before. "I will let him know. Have you thought at all about when you can come back? Or should I make a trip up to The Opulence?"

"As much as I'd love to see you, things are so hectic right now. I'm hoping I can be back in a week."

An entire week. Liam hated that idea, but he understood. "Perhaps we can go out for a nice dinner when you return."

"Or we could eat in," she said, with a very sexy and leading inflection.

"I love the way your mind works."

Teresa laughed, but there was a commotion on the other line, the sound of voices. "I should go. I have a meeting with Aspen about catering for the retreat. It's only a few weeks away."

"You do what you need to do. I'll call you later."

Liam hung up and put his phone on mute, then took a moment to look out the window, the city flying by in a blur while raindrops battered the glass. Even with the scenery, he couldn't keep visions of his dad out of his head. Most sons probably had memories of playing catch or being taught how to ride a bike, but the closest Liam came to that were the times his dad had taken him out on the family yacht. Otherwise, Liam's remembrances were of his dad coming home well after dinner had been served, too tired to do much more than ruffle his son's hair and maybe ask about school. Liam was duly thankful for the hard work his father had put into growing Christopher Corporation. He only wished the man had taken a moment or two to breathe. Which might have had something to with him collapsing. Liam guessed his dad was suffering from exhaustion. It would likely be his job to tell his father to slow down.

The driver pulled up in front of his father's house, the one he bought after he'd divorced Liam's mother. Dad had left the family home to Mom, which had seemed kind at the time, although his mother managed to put it in a bad light, insisting that he'd only done it to stick her with the bad memories of the things that had led to the deterioration of their marriage. Liam had only been to this house five or six times in the five years since the divorce. How sad was that? Liam needed to change that. Maybe his dad's health scare was a wake-up call.

Liam took the stairs two at a time and ducked under cover from the rain. His dad's housekeeper answered quickly.

"Liam. He's waiting for you. He's been asking about you." She turned and led the way down the large central hall, up the right side of the circular staircase and down the corridor to the double doors of his father's bedroom at the very end. With every step closer, the gravity of the situation seemed to bear down on him. This might be life or death. And since his father never remarried and Liam was an only child, he was left alone to deal with it.

The housekeeper opened the door and looked at Liam with entirely too much pity for his liking. "Be sure to speak softly. And don't raise the shades. The light bothers his eyes."

Liam was even more confused now. The day was as gray as could be. But he didn't ask. He just wanted to see his dad.

Ahead, his formidable father looked tiny in the elegantly dressed king-size bed. A nurse was there, checking his pulse. She turned and saw Liam and smiled thinly, as if she couldn't bear to share the bad news. As to what that was, Liam had no idea. He stepped closer and saw that his dad's eyes were shut.

"Is he sleeping?" Liam whispered to the nurse.

She shook her head. "Resting. It hurts his eyes right now. I'll be outside if you need me."

"Wait, I'm sorry. I don't understand. Collapsing hurt his eyes?"

"No." His father's voice was fragile. Like it might break. "Sit down, son. I'll explain."

Liam took the chair next to his bedside, reaching out for his hand. As soon as he touched him, his dad's eyes began to open, but he closed them quickly. "Dad. Talk to me. Are you okay?"

A smile slowly spread across his father's face. Liam had never seen him look so old or frail. This was not the strong man Liam knew. "I don't want you to get angry with me, but I've had a health situation for the past few years that's finally catching up with me."

"What kind of situation?"

"Brain cancer."

Liam suddenly felt like he couldn't breathe. "What? When did this happen? Is that why your eyes hurt?"

His father nodded. "It's pressing on the optic nerve. That part started a few days ago. I've been taking painkillers, but they've stopped working."

"Well, we need to get the best doctors in here right away to see you."

"I've already seen the best doctors. I've been all over the world. Nobody can help me."

Liam was stuck between shock and disbelief. None of this felt real. "Why in the world did you keep this from me? Dad, why didn't you let me know this was going on?"

"I didn't want you to worry, and no father wants to admit to his son that he's not as strong as he's always tried to be. Plus, I didn't want anyone at the company to worry, either. There's nothing like a sick CEO to make everyone panic."

"But I'm your son. Didn't I deserve to know?"

His father nodded and took another peek from under his eyelids. "I thought I could beat it. Nobody likes to feel weak like this. But I have to surrender to it now."

The question was right on Liam's lips but he was terrified to ask. "How long do you have?"

"Days, Liam. That's why I sent for you right away. You're the most important person in my life. I need you to know that I believe in you. You are going to do great things. When you receive your copy of the will, you will see that you will be named CEO. Just as we've always discussed. You can steer the ship. I know I gave you a hard time about the Sasha project, but you were right about it. I never should have doubted you."

Liam squeezed his dad's hand, desperate to hold on to him. "It's okay. I like that we butted heads at work. It made things interesting."

His dad smiled, crinkles forming at the corners of his eyes. "I always admired that you weren't one to back down."

Liam sighed, his heart heavy. He could hardly believe this was happening. "Is there anything else I need to know about the succession plan or the company?"

"No. It's all sewn up, exactly like I told you. I want you to take the helm the instant I'm gone. It'll make for the smoothest transition if you're strong with it. Take command. Don't hesitate."

"I will."

"But there is something else. Something more personal I need to say."

"What's that?"

"Don't make the same mistakes I did. Don't live for your work. Will you promise me you'll fall in love and get married and have a whole litter of Christopher children?"

Liam had never discussed such things with his father, not even when Liam was a teenager and first interested in girls. His mother had given him the sex talk, and like most things with her, it had come with a touch of melodrama. "I'll do my best. I promise."

"Is there a lady in your life, Liam?"

Liam nodded. "There is. It's very new, but I like her a lot. It's actually someone you know. Someone who wanted me to send her best. Teresa St. Claire."

His father lifted his chin and an unusual look crossed his face. "Really? How wonderful. She's a lovely girl. So much drive and determination."

"I know. I get the distinct feeling I should stay out of her way."

His father laughed quietly. "She was the smartest student I've ever had. She understood business on a level that was uncanny. It came naturally to her and all she wanted was to learn more."

"And that's why you took her under your wing?" Liam nearly stopped breathing, waiting for the answer.

"That and I saw something special in her. She was going places. You know, your mother was convinced I had an affair with her. That was the beginning of the end of our marriage. She would never believe me that nothing had ever happened." His father's voice held the same conviction that Teresa's did when she spoke of this subject. Plus, his dad was opening himself up to Liam in a way he never had. He was putting it all on the line. There was no saving face today. There was no reason to lie. "Not that you want my opinion, but I approve of Teresa if she ends up being your wife."

Wife. Liam could only imagine such a thing in the vaguest sense of the word, like seeing a ghost or a mirage off in the distance. His parents had such a dysfunctional marriage. Seemingly loveless. Could he get it right? Or was he doomed to make the same mistakes? "That's good to know, Dad. I appreciate it."

The nurse stepped into the room. "Mr. Christopher, it's time for your pain medication."

His dad nodded. "Just one more minute with my son."

Liam took his dad's hand. "I'll come and see you tomorrow, okay? In the morning? We can have breakfast and talk some more." With his dad fading, Liam wanted to get everything he could out of these final days, especially with him being so open and honest. Liam had been waiting for that his entire life.

"I'd like that. Very much."

Liam rose and leaned down to kiss his father on the forehead. "I love you, Dad."

"I love you, too, son."

As he walked out of the room, Liam managed a smile at the nurse. Right before a tear rolled down his cheek.

Fourteen

Matt had been avoiding the office for an entire week, finding any excuse to meet people for lunch or coffee, any reason to hop in his car and drive to Portland or…anywhere other than Richmond Industries headquarters. It was simply too painful to walk past Nadia's desk several times a day and see someone else sitting there. All he could think about was how much better Nadia made his day with her beauty, brains and generous ways. Braydon, the temporary assistant HR had sent over, was competent, and he'd probably work out once he got up to speed, but he was also a stark reminder of who was no longer sitting outside Matt's office.

But he couldn't stay away today. It was Monday

morning, which meant the weekly meeting with key staff. He had to steer the ship or at least nudge it in the right direction. The retreat was less than two weeks away. There were a million things to do. He was stressed, too. Liam had called a few days ago to tell him that his father was gravely ill. This had come as a shock to Matt, but Liam had sounded as if he'd been hit by a truck. They'd been talking every day since then. Matt mostly just listened as Liam tried to process what was happening.

Matt's phone rang and he was relieved to see it was Liam. "Hey, buddy. How are you doing? How's your dad?"

"He's gone, Matt. He died. Early this morning. I didn't even get to talk to him again. He was too sick to see me yesterday. I showed up at his house and I just got turned away."

Matt dropped his elbow onto his desk and kneaded his forehead. "Man, I am so sorry. Tell me where you are. I'll come to see you. I don't think you should be alone."

"No. No. It's fine. I'm at work and everyone is freaking out. People are crying. Hell, I had to send half of the accounting department home because they were so upset. I need to stay and keep things together. My dad was very clear about this. Everyone at the company needs to be reminded of the succession plan. They need to know that the transfer of power is instantaneous and seamless. They can't see me be anything but calm and collected."

Matt shook his head and leaned back in his chair. "Liam, your father just passed away. It's okay for you to feel bad or show some emotion right now. Nobody is going to blame you."

The other end of the line was quiet and that made it feel like Matt's heart was being ripped out. "I can't. I have to hold everything together."

This was so true of Liam. His family, the business— he kept it all together. But who was going to keep Liam together? "That's what you do, isn't it? You keep everything together."

"I don't have a choice."

Matt sighed, resigned to the fact that he would never convince Liam to take a break. Not today. Perhaps it was best for him to soldier through the next eight hours and leave his grieving for home, where he could be alone.

Braydon poked his head into Matt's office. "I'm sorry to interrupt, but Teresa St. Claire is on the line. She says it's urgent."

Matt nodded and held up a finger to let Braydon know he needed a minute. "Hey, Liam. Teresa is on the other line. I think she's out at The Opulence, so I should probably take her call. It's probably about the retreat."

"Yeah. Yeah. Of course. Tell her I say hi."

How things had changed in a few short weeks. "How are things between you two?"

"Good. Fine."

"Is there a love connection there?"

"Love? No. We're friends."

Matt didn't want to press Liam any further. That could wait until later. Plus, Teresa was on the line. "Okay. I'll call you later to check on you." Matt ended the call on his cell and picked up his office line. "Teresa. How can I help you?"

"Can you tell me what your relationship is like with your brother?"

Matt nearly laughed, especially thinking about the horrible things that had transpired at his parents' house. "You have a few hundred hours for me to explain? Let's just say that it's adversarial at best. Why do you ask?"

"He was here at The Opulence over the weekend. He made a bit of an impression on the staff. Drinking too much in the bar and, honestly, talking trash about you a fair amount. One of the bartenders said he bragged last night that he was behind the *TBG* stories."

Matt wasn't entirely surprised. Zach took any chance he could to embarrass Matt or make him look bad. Of course, he'd chosen one of Richmond Industries' most exclusive properties to smear his name. "Thank you for sharing, but I already knew about it. He threatened me with it the night I thought I was bringing Nadia to meet my parents. My brother basically broke Nadia and I up because of it."

"Well, that's not all your brother said. He was railing on Shayla, calling her a snake and saying that she'd forced him to do it. Something about blackmail and forcing Nadia out."

Matt froze in his seat. He could hardly believe what he was hearing. "Do you trust this bartender?"

"I do. I've spent a lot of time trying to get to know the staff. And it wasn't just the bartender who overheard. Aspen heard him say something, and so did Isabel Withers, the concierge. I wouldn't call you if I wasn't certain there was something to the story."

Matt was struggling to put this all together. "Why in the world would Shayla do that? She's one of my most trusted employees."

"I don't know, Matt. You'll have to ask her yourself. And then I think you need to speak to Nadia."

Oh, God. Nadia. She might kill Shayla with her small but capable hands if it turned out that she was behind the tabloid stories. "Thanks for this info. I really appreciate it."

"No problem. Have you heard from Liam?"

"I have. He told me about his dad."

"It's so sad. He called me early this morning, right after it happened. He's so upset. I'm trying to convince him to come relax for a few days out at The Opulence, but he's all wrapped up in the succession plan and the lawyers and the will." So there *was* a love connection between Liam and Teresa. "I'm hoping to see him tomorrow."

"Great. I'm sure he could use the company. And thank you for calling. I really appreciate it." Matt said goodbye to Teresa and called out to Braydon. "Can you get Shayla in here right away?"

Braydon nodded and picked up his phone, then sprang over to Matt's door. "She's on her way."

Matt got up from his desk and began pacing his office, going over the events of the last few weeks. It all made sense now, except that it didn't. He couldn't imagine what her motive would be. Why would she want to hurt the company she worked for? What could she possibly be blackmailing Zach with?

He didn't need to ask himself these questions for long, though. Shayla turned up in his doorway. "Braydon said you needed me."

Matt just looked at her, shaking his head in disbelief. "I need to ask you something and I need complete honesty."

"Of course. You always get the truth from me."

Matt was starting to think that might not be the case. "Are you behind the *TBG* stories? Are you blackmailing my brother?"

He waited for her to defend herself or blurt out that he was wrong, but she did nothing of the sort. Instead, she wandered over to one of the chairs opposite his desk and sat down. "I guess I'm not completely surprised that you found out, but I was hoping that I'd gotten away with it. Nadia's been gone for an entire week and the office is already a better place."

"What in the hell are you talking about?"

Shayla turned to him. "You weren't yourself when she was here. She was a distraction."

"That is not true. And who put you in charge? It's not your place to pull these kinds of strings behind the scenes."

She shook her head and looked down at her lap. "It's your fault, you know. It's not like I didn't try. Every day, Matt. Working hard. Dressing impeccably. Being at your beck and call. If you'd just noticed me, this never would have happened."

"Noticed you? I notice you all the time. You're a complete pain in my ass, but you're a great employee. What exactly were you wanting from me?"

She turned back to him then slowly rose out of the chair. "You. I wanted you, Matt. All that time I was with Zach, it was just to get closer to you. Why do you think I've stayed all these years?" She approached him like a tiger hiding in the tall grass, stalking her prey. "I've had a million job offers. I've had other companies throw money at me. But no, I stayed, because I kept hoping that you would wake up one day and see me as the woman who loves you."

Matt felt his eyes go wide with surprise. He had *not* seen this coming. "You told Zach that I was bringing Nadia to have dinner with our parents."

She kept approaching and Matt started backing up, wanting to stay away. "I had to do something. I heard that pathetic confession you made to Nadia at Gideon's party. I couldn't let you throw everything away like that. Zach had been calling me for weeks, trying to see if I could help him convince you to bring him back on board with the company. I decided to turn the tables on him and ask for a favor in return. As you know, an old friend of his owns *TBG*. I had to make him do the dirty work."

"What could you possibly blackmail Zach with?"

Shayla laughed. "Let me guess. He told you that he's cleaned up his act. Well, he hasn't. He's just as messed up as ever and has a ton of gambling debts. That's the real reason he's back pulling on the family purse strings. He needs the money."

It all made sense now. Of course Zach hadn't really put himself back together. He'd merely managed to make it look as though he had. The trouble was that he could never seem to do anything without making threats. That had always been one of his biggest downfalls. "Shayla, I'm your boss. I've never had a single romantic thought about you. I don't know why you would think I would. It's not appropriate."

Her jaw tightened. "Oh, you're my boss? Now you care about what's appropriate? You were willing to cross that line for Nadia, but you weren't willing to cross it for me?"

"Nadia was different." As soon as he'd said it and he heard his own words, he knew that Nadia was, indeed, different. He loved her. She was the only woman for him. And if he didn't act quickly, he might lose her forever. "Braydon," he called. "Get Security up here. Now."

Suddenly Shayla was like an animal backed into a corner. "You're calling Security on me? I will take you down, Matt Richmond. Even if I have to use Zach to do it."

"You can't hurt me any more than you already have, Shayla. You made me lose the woman I love."

For the first time during their exchange, Shayla looked truly hurt. "You love her?"

"I do. And now I'm going to beg her to take me back." He marched out of the room just as two members of the security team arrived. He looked back at Shayla, feeling nothing but pity for her. "Get her out of here. She's fired."

Nadia had not done well with her brief unemployment. It was not a break, nor was it a vacation. She tried to sleep in, but she only tossed and turned. She'd tried long walks and marathon trips to the gym, but those didn't help, either, especially when she saw people covering their mouths and whispering about her. It seemed that this time, everyone in Seattle had seen the tabloid dirt. This was what her life had become—she was blacklisted.

Even her family was embarrassed. She'd hoped they wouldn't find out about the tabloid story, but they had, and when they called her on it, some terrible words had come up. Words like *shameful*. Her parents were glad she'd quit Matt's company and begged her to come back to California, where she could get a normal job and live a quiet life. It was the last thing Nadia wanted. She knew there were professional challenges for her in Seattle. But she needed someone to take a chance on her and that person was Teresa. So, on her third day away from Richmond Industries, Nadia called Teresa and asked if she could have a trial employment period with Limitless Events.

She asked for no pay, and although she was willing to work on the Richmond retreat, she wanted to do it behind the scenes. No one could know what she was doing, or where she was working, which was with Teresa. And that meant at The Opulence. Mostly she didn't want Matt to know.

He hadn't reached out once in the week they'd been apart, which was a good thing, but it had all changed today. In fact, he'd called three times and it was only early afternoon. She missed him terribly, but she was resigned to her fate and she wasn't going to call him back. She wouldn't even listen to the messages. They could be friends someday, but even with all of their work troubles aside, he wasn't prepared to give her what she wanted. He wasn't a man who was looking for the long haul. The sooner she learned to live with that, the better off she'd be.

Nadia was hunkered down in one of The Opulence meeting rooms with seating charts for the various meals to be served during the retreat when

Teresa walked in. "Is there something wrong with your phone?" she asked.

Nadia picked it up and looked at it. Another message from Matt. "No. Matt keeps calling, so I haven't been answering it."

"Why? Don't want to talk to him?"

"What is there to say? Even with our work problems aside, he's not a commitment kind of guy, and that's all I've ever wanted. It's best if we stay away from each other for a while."

Teresa blew out a breath. "Well, I'm sorry, but I'm afraid that I outed you. He called me an hour ago and asked if I knew where you were, so I told him."

"You did what?"

Teresa shrugged. "Sorry. He insisted. He said it was life or death. He's on his way here right now."

Nadia got up from the table, now in a panic. She wasn't prepared to see Matt. She was wearing a very plain black skirt and boring white blouse and her hair was so frizzy from being around Centennial Falls all the time. "What do I do?"

"Go out to the lobby, wait for him to arrive and see what he has to say?"

Nadia stormed past Teresa and out into the hall. "That's not super helpful."

"Sorry. I'm no relationship expert. Ask anyone."

"Oh, my God. I can't believe this is happening." Nadia strode down the hall, her heart threatening to pound its way out of her throat. She had to prepare herself for what Matt might say. If he asked to get back together, she was going to have to stay strong and say no. And if he asked her something else, well, she couldn't imagine what that might be, so she'd just have to wing it. It then occurred to her that he might simply need something work-related. But that didn't make sense, either. Why would a guy as busy as Matt drive all the way out to The Opulence to ask her a question?

She was heading for the lobby when she heard a voice behind her.

A voice that made her clamp her eyes shut as a million feelings came roaring back to life. "Nadia. I've been looking for you everywhere."

She turned, and the minute she laid eyes on Matt, the notion of being strong went right out the window. She'd have to fake it. "What are you doing here?" Knowing that if she got any closer to him, she'd only get weaker, she stood her ground.

It was Matt who closed the gap between them. "I left you messages. Shayla was behind everything, not Zach." He looked down at the ground and stuffed his hands into his pockets. "Actually, Zach still played his part, but Shayla blackmailed him. So she could get rid of you."

"What did I ever do to her?" Nadia was still trying to catch up to the things Matt had just said.

"It was my fault. She said she was in love with me and had been for years. I know it sounds crazy, but you were the one who got in the way."

Nadia had to laugh, even though it was a short-lived chuckle. "I told you she had it for you." She took zero solace in being right. "I'm glad you figured out the mystery. At least I know now why I lost my job."

"You could come back if you wanted to."

She shook her head, thankful Teresa had taken a chance on her. It made it easier to say no to Matt. "I'm working for Limitless now. It's on a trial basis, but Teresa and I work well together. I think it's going to be good for me."

"I am so happy to hear that. You're going to do an amazing job." His eyes filled with hope, and that made Nadia's heart sink. She loved Matt. She didn't want him to think there was a chance. "Which brings me to the subject of us and back to the subject of Shayla."

"You know I had to leave for reasons that go way beyond Shayla. Your family, and your willingness to commit. Both huge problems."

Matt was quick to shake his head. He took her hand. "First off, I called my parents right after I talked to Shayla. They can't believe what she and Zach got up to. They feel terrible that he lied to everyone. They feel terrible for you. They want to meet you. For real. Just the four of us. No creepy brothers allowed."

Nadia smiled. This was so sweet, and a few weeks ago this would have been the best news ever. "That's nice to hear, but—"

"No. Wait. Hold on. Let me get the rest of this

out. Because the rest of this is all on me. I love you, Nadia Gonzalez. I love you more than words can explain. And I'm sorry that I didn't say that while we were together, but I'm saying it now. I realized it this morning after all of the craziness with Shayla. That's why I've been calling. That's why I left messages and drove all the way up here."

Nadia didn't move. She couldn't speak. Hell, she could hardly blink. "You love me? I love you, too."

A purely happy smile crossed his face. "I love you so much that I can't ever let you go. I can't let you out of my sight. I want you forever." And then Matt Richmond, the man she had once thought could never be for her, knelt and looked up into her eyes, holding her hand tightly and filling her with so much love and optimism that she thought her heart might burst. "Will you stay with me forever? Will you be my wife?"

"Yes. Oh, my God. Yes." She tugged on his hand. "Now get up here and kiss me."

Matt stood and swept her into his arms, holding her so tightly that he lifted her feet off the ground. The kiss was warm and soft and absolutely perfect. He was the man she loved and she had him. Forever.

Somewhere off in the distance, she heard applause, which she was sure was just her heart, but then Matt set her back on the floor and she turned to see the lobby full of people clapping. Isabel, Aspen, Teresa, the guys from the valet stand, the bellhops and guests had seen it all. Nadia couldn't even be embarrassed. She was just too happy.

"Congratulations." Teresa gave them each a hug, then took Nadia's hand. "No ring, Matt?"

Matt's shoulders dropped. "I know, I know. I should have come prepared, but I didn't want to wait." He then turned to Nadia and took her hand, bringing it to his lips. "Plus, you should have the chance to pick out whatever you want. I was thinking Tiffany's. In New York."

Was this really her life now? Wow. "Uh, sure. That sounds amazing. I guess we could go sometime after the retreat."

He shook his head. "I was thinking tomorrow night. I have a few things I need to catch up on, but I want you to have a ring as soon as possible. We'll just go for a day or two."

Nadia turned to Teresa. "Is that going to be okay with you? I just started work."

Teresa smiled. "Of course. Who am I to stand in the way of true love?"

Fifteen

Teresa had to admit that watching Matt profess his love for Nadia had certainly put her in a romantic mood. It had been such a sweet moment, and it was so nice to see things work out for them. Today they would be flying off to New York so Matt could take Nadia to Tiffany & Co. for a ring. Teresa would've been jealous if she didn't have her own prize waiting for her back in Seattle. Her dinner with Liam.

She'd been in the car for about a half hour when he called. "Hello?" she answered over the speakerphone.

"So there's a slight change of plans if that's okay."

"I'm already on my way back."

"We're still having dinner. But not at my place.

I was hoping we could take out my boat. It was one of the few things my dad and I used to do together and I thought it would be a good way to honor his memory." Just when she was about to mention that she was not much of a fisherman, he continued. "It's nice. I promise. You'll be comfortable."

Honestly, all she wanted was to see him and pick up where they'd left off. "Okay, great."

"Also, you should know that I have my copy of my dad's will and I'm waiting until tonight to open it."

"Why would you wait?"

"It's going to be emotional and I wanted to be away from the office and my house when I did it. Plus, my dad liked you a lot. That means something."

Teresa sighed. She really enjoyed this softer side of Liam. "That all sounds wonderful. Just tell me where to meet you."

"I'll text you the info. How long will you be?"

"I'm a half hour away now. Do I have time to go home and change?"

"I don't really see the point. You won't be wearing clothes for long."

A smile crossed Teresa lips and she ran her fingers along the stitching on the steering wheel. "You make a compelling case. I'll come straight over."

"Good. I can't wait."

Teresa hung up, but found her phone ringing again right away with an unknown number. She really needed a break, but that would have to come after the retreat. For now, she had to answer. "Hello?"

"Hey, sis."

She sat a little straighter in her seat. "Joshua. How are you? Is everything okay?" She hadn't received any more phone calls after Liam's guy checked on Josh. *Please let nothing be wrong now.*

"Everything is fine. I've got everything worked out. Just stop checking on me all the time, okay?"

"Well, maybe if you'd called me back on a more regular basis, I wouldn't need to do that."

"I'm busy, okay. I'm working. I have to have a job, you know."

"Does this job involve things that are legal?" She couldn't take it if Joshua ended up in jail. She'd worked so hard to keep him out. And, of course, she could only imagine trying to explain it to her mother. Teresa was responsible one way or another, whether she liked it or not.

"Yes. I promise. Everything is fine." He sighed heavily. "Look, I know you've always been there for me, but you're not Mom. I can take care of myself. At some point, you're going to have to trust me to do what's right."

A little piece of Teresa felt like it was dying. She'd cared for her brother for as long as she could remember. Forget responsibility. It was her instinct to do it. "I know. I hope you can appreciate why I want to protect you. I love you." Tears began to well at the corners of her eyes.

"I love you, too. Everything is going to be fine. I promise."

His voice was clear and strong and that made her want to believe that things really would be okay. "Good. I'm glad to hear it."

"Cool. Well, I have stuff to do. I'll try to call more often. Bye."

"Bye." Teresa hung up and was overcome with a feeling she didn't have very often—calm. Things were working out. They were falling into place. Who knew that was even possible? Her phone beeped with the text from Liam. She clicked on the link and it pulled up the navigation for Shilshole Bay Marina.

When she arrived, Teresa parked her car, grabbed her Fendi bag and a jacket and made her way over to the docks. There was a wide array of boats out, but no sign of Liam until she heard him shouting her name. "Teresa! Over here!"

She turned and he was at the far end, standing at the end of a gangplank next to quite possibly the largest yacht she had ever seen. She rushed up to him, nearly running in heels. He was smiling and when he swiped off his sunglasses, his intense gaze met hers. For a moment, the rest of the world faded away. The seabirds overhead, the other people on the docks and the hum of the marina became nothing more than a blurry backdrop. Her entire focus was Liam. She savored the sexy way he refused to let their connection drop. It was a thunderbolt straight to the heart.

"How are you?" he asked, grasping her elbows and placing a soft kiss on her lips.

"I'm great. Also, you are a liar. This is not a boat. This is more like a floating city."

He laughed and put his sunglasses back on. "Just wait until you get on board. Then I'll really blow your mind." His hand settled on the small of her back and he ushered her across the gangplank, where a deckhand stood sentry at the very end.

"Wow," Teresa said when she stepped down onto the main deck. "How big is this thing?"

"It's a sixty-eight-meter BNow. Three upper decks above the main deck, two lower—one for me and guests, one for the staff. There's a hot tub and a table for ten out on the aft deck."

Teresa walked ahead with Liam by her side, the wind in her hair as she admired her surroundings. This was just absolutely stunning, with a glossy wood deck and gleaming chrome. Pure luxury with a large outdoor seating area filled with inviting loungers and colorful pillows. Beyond was the hot tub he'd mentioned, which would afford fabulous sea views. With all of it set against the beautiful backdrop of deep blue sea and the slowly setting sun, it felt nothing short of both lavish and romantic. It was like stepping into an instant vacation. And with an incredibly sexy man, to boot.

"Come inside," he said, taking her hand again. "We have champagne and I have something I want to ask you."

Liam had already surprised her greatly with the yacht. She couldn't imagine what else he had in store. But as he tugged on her hand, urging her to join him, she knew she was prepared for anything this man had to offer. Anything at all.

Just as the boat was leaving the dock, Liam led Teresa into the main living space on the boat, an expansive living room with a sleek modern sectional sofa and a huge television, although there was no point in ever turning it on. The 360-degree view from that room was the real focus. Of course, now Liam was focused on gathering his strength to ask Teresa the question he'd been pondering. But first, champagne.

He unwrapped the foil and popped the cork on a bottle of Krug, then filled two flutes. He offered one to Teresa and held his for a toast. "To my father."

She smiled warmly. "Yes. To your father. He raised an amazing son."

Liam took a sip, appreciating Teresa's sentiment, but unsure he could really live up to a label like amazing. Losing his dad was making him see everything through a very different lens, but the good side of that was he knew he needed to focus on his life outside work. Hopefully a life that could include Teresa.

"You had a question?" she asked, perching on the back of the sofa.

He took a deep breath. "Yes. But first I want to say that I like you, Teresa. I have launched some terrible accusations at you, and not always been on my best behavior and you weren't afraid to stand up to me."

She arched an eyebrow at him, her blue eyes shifting to a darker shade. "I had to defend myself. And I couldn't live with you believing those things about me."

"Absolutely. As it should be. But when you're a man in my position, not many people challenge you. And I think I need that. So, thank you." He swallowed hard. "And so I wanted to ask if you'd be interested in us staying together during the retreat at The Opulence. We'll both be incredibly busy, but I think we both know we'll have a hard time staying away from each other."

"I'll definitely need to blow off some steam."

He took her hand and raised it to his lips. "Take it all out on me. Please."

She stood and led him over to the sofa, where they sat close. "I like you, too, Liam. A lot. You might be the most complex man I've ever met."

A breathy laugh escaped his lips. "That's a good thing?"

"It makes me want to dig past the layers to find the real you."

Liam's fingers went to her jaw and her eyes met his. "I hope you find what you're looking for." He kissed her softly, relishing the way she nearly melted into him. It made him so eager for more time alone with her.

From across the room, Liam heard someone clear their throat. He and Teresa quickly separated, both a bit startled. It was the chief steward, standing with his hands behind his back. "Mr. Christopher, I'm sorry to interrupt, but dinner will be served in an hour."

"Great. Thank you."

"I guess there's no real privacy on a boat, huh?" Teresa asked, sitting back and sipping more of her champagne.

"There will be. Later." Liam glanced down at the coffee table and the thick envelope waiting for him. He hadn't even peeked inside. Something had told him that it wasn't a good idea to be alone when he read the documents, but Matt was leaving for New York this evening with Nadia, and Teresa had indeed been close to his dad. "I guess I'll take this chance to take a look at my dad's will. Get it over with. It won't take long."

Teresa nodded eagerly. "Yes. Of course. Open it."

Liam sat back and opened the flap, pulling out the thick sheaf of papers. "Just a little light reading," he joked.

"Anything in particular you're looking for?"

He began flipping through the pages. "No. Not really. My dad and I discussed it the day he told me he was sick. So I think I know pretty much everything. Of course, I have to make sure it's all in order."

"Of course. A lot of money on the line."

"And the company." Liam leaned forward and took another drink, then went back to reading. "I hope I'm not boring you with this."

Teresa reached out and rubbed his shoulder affectionately. "It's not boring to me. This is your future. And your past. I'm honored to be a part of it. It makes me feel good to know you wanted to include me."

Liam began looking through the personal assets. The vacation house in Bali. His father's yacht, which was moored in the Cayman Islands. The winery and villa in Tuscany. "There's a lot of property on this list. I'm going to need to hire someone just to deal with all of it."

Teresa's eyes lit up. "Ooh. Like what?"

Liam's sights returned to the document. "Mountain house in Switzerland? How does that strike you?"

She patted his leg. "Sounds lovely. Now which way to the ladies' room?" She got up from her seat and Liam pointed her in the direction the steward had taken.

"Right back there. First door on the right."

"Perfect. I'll be right back."

Liam's phone beeped with a text and he pulled it out of his pocket. It was from Matt, a photo of Nadia and him on Matt's jet. Just like he and Teresa, they were toasting with champagne. The message read:

On our way to the Big Apple. See you in two days.

Liam couldn't help but smile at his phone. It felt so damn good to know that Matt had found happiness. True love, no less. Could Liam have that ahead? Was it possible? One step at a time, of course, but it was hard not to think he was on the right track with Teresa.

He tapped out a reply to Matt.

Have fun. Love you guys.

Liam returned to his reading and the long list of personal effects. His father or his lawyer had been very thorough. There were pages and pages of watches and cars and plots of land all over the world. Impatient, Liam flipped ahead to the sections about the business. He just wanted to make sure that everything was in order, that he'd explained the succession plan accurately and that there were no surprises. The stability of the company, especially in light of the passing of its founder and CEO, was of paramount importance.

But when he reached the section where it was supposed to say that one hundred percent of his father's personal stake of the company went to Liam, there was a single detail he had never, ever imagined. Something that made it feel like his heart had not only stopped, but that it might also not ever beat again.

75% of personal stake in Christopher Corporation to Liam Christopher

And...

25% of personal stake in Christopher Corporation to Teresa St. Claire

Teresa returned from the bathroom, looking refreshed. "What'd I miss?"

Liam felt sick. Truly, truly sick. Everything that had been so perfect a few seconds ago had just gone up in smoke. He closed his eyes and took a deep breath before saying what he had to say. "I can't believe you lied to me."

* * * * *

How will Liam and Teresa deal with his father's betrayal? Is Joshua really on the hook for millions? What happens when a storm rocks the resort?

Don't miss a single episode in the Dynasties: Secrets of the A-List quartet!

Book One
Tempted by Scandal *by Karen Booth*

Book Two
Taken by Storm *by Cat Schield*
Available June 2019

Book Three
Seduced by Second Chances *by Reese Ryan*
Available July 2019

Book Four
Redeemed by Passion *by Joss Wood*
Available August 2019

#2665 HIS TO CLAIM
The Westmoreland Legacy • by Brenda Jackson
Honorary Westmoreland Thurston "Mac" McRoy delayed a romantic ranch vacation with his wife for too long—she went without him! Now it will take all his skills to rekindle their desire and win back his wife...

#2666 RANCHER IN HER BED
Texas Cattleman's Club: Houston • by Joanne Rock
Rich rancher Xander Currin isn't looking for a relationship. Cowgirl Frankie Walsh won't settle for anything less. When combustible desire consumes them both just as secrets from Frankie's past come to light, will their passion survive?

#2667 TAKEN BY STORM
Dynasties: Secrets of the A-List • by Cat Schield
Isabel Withers knows her boss, hotel executive Shane Adams, should be off-limits—but the chances he'll notice her are zilch. Until they're stranded together in a storm and let passion rule. Can their forbidden love overcome the scandals waiting for them?

#2668 THE BILLIONAIRE'S BARGAIN
Blackout Billionaires • by Naima Simone
Chicago billionaire Darius King never surrenders...until a blackout traps him with an irresistible beauty. Then the light reveals his enemy—his late best friend's widow! Marriage is the only way to protect his friend's legacy, but soon her secrets will force Darius to question everything...

#2669 FROM MISTAKE TO MILLIONS
Switched! • by Andrea Laurence
A DNA kit just proved Jade Nolan is *not* a Nolan. Desperate for answers, she accepts the help of old flame Harley Dalton—even though she knows she can't resist him. What will happen when temptation leads to passion and the truth complicates everything?

#2670 STAR-CROSSED SCANDAL
Plunder Cove • by Kimberley Troutte
When Chloe Harper left Hollywood to reunite with her family, she vowed to heal herself before hooking up with *anyone*. But now sexy star-maker Nicolas Medeiros is at her resort, offering her the night of her dreams. She takes it...and more. But how will she let him go?

SPECIAL EXCERPT FROM

HQN™

*Beatrix Leighton has loved Gold Valley cowboy
Dane Parker from afar for years, and she's about to
discover that forbidden love might just be the sweetest...*

Read on for a sneak preview of
Unbroken Cowboy
by New York Times *and* USA TODAY
bestselling author Maisey Yates.

It was her first kiss. But that didn't matter.

It was Dane. That was all that mattered. That was all that really mattered.

Dane, the man she'd fantasized about a hundred times—maybe a thousand times—doing this very thing. But this was so much brighter and more vivid than a fantasy could ever be. Color and texture and taste. The rough whiskers on his face, the heat of his breath, the way those big, sure hands cupped her face as his lips moved slowly over hers.

She took a step and the shattered glass crunched beneath her feet, but she didn't care. She didn't care at all. She wanted to breathe in this moment for as long as she could, broken glass be damned. To exist just like this, with his lips against hers, for as long as she possibly could.

She leaned forward, wrapped her fingers around the fabric of his T-shirt and clung to him, holding them both steady, because she was afraid she might fall if she didn't.

Her knees were weak. Like in a book or a movie.

She hadn't known that kissing could really, literally, make your knees weak. Or that touching a man you wanted could make you feel like you were burning up, like you had a fever. Could make you feel hollow and restless and desperate for what came next...

Even if what came next scared her a little.

It was Dane.

She trusted Dane.

With her secrets. With her body.

Dane.

She breathed his name on a whispered sigh as she moved to take their kiss deeper, and found herself being set back, glass crunching beneath her feet yet again.

"I should go," he said, his voice rough.

"No!" The denial burst out of her, and she found herself reaching forward to grab his shirt again. "No," she said again, this time a little less crazy and desperate.

She didn't feel any less crazy and desperate.

"I have to go, Bea."

"You don't. You could stay."

The look he gave her burned her down to the soles of her feet. "I can't."

"If you're worried about… I didn't misunderstand. I mean I know that if you stayed we would…"

"Dammit, Bea," he bit out. "We can't. You know that."

"Why? I'm not stupid. I know you don't want… I don't want…" She stumbled over her words because it all seemed stupid. To say something as inane as she knew they wouldn't get married. Even saying it made her feel like a silly virgin.

She was a virgin. There wasn't really any glossing over that. But she didn't have to seem silly.

She did know, though. For all that everyone saw her as soft and naive, she wasn't. She'd carried a torch for Dane for a long time but she'd also realistically seen how marriage worked. Her brother was a cheater. Her mother was a cheater.

Her father was… She didn't even know.

That was the legacy of love and marriage in her family.

Truly, she didn't want any part of it.

Some companionship, though. Sex. She wanted that. With him. Why couldn't she have that? McKenna made it sound simple, and possible. And Bea wanted it.

Don't miss
Unbroken Cowboy *by Maisey Yates,*
available May 2019 wherever Harlequin® books
and ebooks are sold.

www.Harlequin.com

Thurston McRoy, called Mac by all who knew him, still had
his arms around his mother's shoulders when he felt her tense
up. "Mom? You okay?" he asked, looking down at her.

When his parents glanced over at each other, that uneasy
feeling from earlier crept over him again. Not liking it, he
turned to go down the hall toward his bedroom when his father
reached out to stop him.

"Teri isn't here, Mac."

Mac turned back to his father. His mother had moved to
stand beside his dad.

"It's after two in the morning and tomorrow is a school day
for the girls. So where is she?"

His mother reached out and touched his arm. "She needed
to get away and she asked if we would come keep the girls."

Mac frowned. He knew his wife. She would not have gone
anywhere without their daughters. "What do you mean, she
needed to get away? Why?"

"She's the one who has to tell you that, Thurston. It's not
for us to say."

HDEXP0519

Mac drew in a deep breath, not understanding any of this. Because his parents were acting so secretive, he felt his confusion and anger escalating. "Fine. Where is she?"

It was his father who spoke. "She left three days ago for the Torchlight Dude Ranch."

Mac's frown deepened. "The Torchlight Dude Ranch? In Wyoming?"

"Yes."

"What the hell did she go there for?"

His father didn't say anything for a minute and then gave Mac an answer. "She said she always wanted to go back there."

Mac rubbed his hand across his face. Yes, Teri had always wanted to go back there, the place he'd taken her on their honeymoon, a little over ten years ago. And he'd always promised to take her back. But between his covert missions and their growing family, there had never been enough time. Teri, who'd been raised on a ranch in Texas, was a cowgirl at heart and had once dreamed of being on the rodeo circuit due to her roping and riding skills. She'd even represented the state of Texas as a rodeo queen years ago.

When they'd married, she had given it all up to travel around the world with her naval husband. She'd said she'd done so gladly. Why in the world would Teri leave their kids and go to a dude ranch by herself?

He knew the only person who could answer that question was Teri.

It was time to go find his wife.

His to Claim
by New York Times *bestselling author Brenda Jackson, available June 2019 wherever Harlequin® Desire books and ebooks are sold.*

www.Harlequin.com

Love Harlequin romance?

DISCOVER.

Be the first to find out about promotions, news and exclusive content!

Facebook.com/HarlequinBooks

Twitter.com/HarlequinBooks

Instagram.com/HarlequinBooks

Pinterest.com/HarlequinBooks

ReaderService.com

EXPLORE.

Sign up for the Harlequin e-newsletter and download a free book from any series at **TryHarlequin.com.**

CONNECT.

Join our Harlequin community to share your thoughts and connect with other romance readers!
Facebook.com/groups/HarlequinConnection

**ROMANCE WHEN
YOU NEED IT**

HSOCIAL2018